P.O.W.

by

Gloria Darlene Beers

DORRANCE PUBLISHING CO., INC.
PITTSBURGH, PENNSYLVANIA 15222

ISBN # 0-8059-6330-8
Printed in the United States of America

First Printing

For information or to order additional books, please write:
Dorrance Publishing Co., Inc.
701 Smithfield Street
Third Floor
Pittsburgh, Pennsylvania 15222
U.S.A.
1-800-788-7654
Or visit our web site and on-line catalog at www.dorrancepublishing.com

Gloria Darlene Beers

Dedication

I would like to dedicate this book to Kenneth Theodore Linch, whose financial help was invaluable.

Chapter One

M<small>Y NAME IS</small> L<small>LOYD</small> K<small>ING</small>. I <small>WAS BORN ON</small> July 6, 1920, in Hagerman, Chaves County, New Mexico. This is a testimony of my experiences in a Japanese prison camp during World War II. I was one of the longest-held civilian prisoners during that conflict.

It was the beginning of December 1941. I had been working on Wake Island for nine months. I was planning a vacation to return home for the Christmas holidays.

I was told that a company in San Francisco made walking canes from sharks' backbones, and I could sell the bones there for forty-five dollars each. The extra money I dreamed of making was my incentive for harvesting them. That and the abundance of sharks that always presented a threat to the men who enjoyed the delights of the sea. (In reality sharks did not have a hard backbone but a very big strong cartilage, a translucent elastic tissue. After the cartilage weathered it became as hard as bone.)

I had three large bundles of shark backbones stored under my bed to take home, and I could not believe it when I discovered that someone had stolen one bundle from me. I wondered about the intelligence of the thief. What could he have been thinking? Everyone on Wake island knew I was the only one harvesting shark backbones. After all, we were on an island, and a small one at that. Where was the thief going to escape and where was he going to hide them so someone would not see them?

Actually Wake Island consisted of three very tiny atoll islands. The main island was discovered in 1568 by a Spaniard, Slvaro de Mendana, who named it San Francisco. However, not finding any food or water, Captain Mendana was very disappointed and did not recognoze the great value of the island. It was not until 1796 that Captain Samuel Wake visited the island

1

and made the world aware of its prime location. Since then the name *Wake* was assigned to the island. It was not until 1840 that Commodore Wilkes, on a scientific survey conducted by naturalist Titan Peale, that the other two islets were named after these gentlemen.

It was not until 1898 that Major General Francis Green raised the American flag on Wake Island. Then in 1899 the United States took formal possession of Wake Island. And finally on December 29, 1934, Wake Island was placed under the jurisdiction of the United States Navy.

The main island is Wake with a man-made bridge connecting it to Peale Island. Wilkes Island was still undeveloped and separated by a narrow channel that led into a large lagoon. The channel had to be crossed by ferry, which in reality was a small tugboat converted into a ferry. That channel was being enlarged to make room for submarines. The United States government was constructing a military refueling base there. Because Wake Island was the largest, they referred to all of the islands as Wake Island.

Not many days had passed before a friend told me that he knew who had my shark backbones. Even though I wanted those bones returned, I did not feel the bones were worth having any violence over. After all, it was not as if there was a shortage of sharks, and I planned on staying on the island until the work I was assigned to do was finished. By then I would probably have more bones than I could carry, anyway. I decided to confront the thief the following day and tell him I knew of his crime.

I did not have an aggressive nature, and I tossed and turned all night thinking about the best way to handle the situation without confrontation. I searched every corner of my mind to find the proper words to use. My goal was to make him feel so ashamed that he would want to give up his errant ways and never steal anything, ever again.

It was five-thirty in the morning and time for me to get up and face the joys of a new day. I still didn't know what to say to the thief and hoped the proper words would come when I saw him. I dressed quickly and drove to pick up Johnny McCloud. He had been assigned to work with me. We had a good working relationship even though we had not worked together for very long.

There were a few small houses that had been built upon stilts for the bosses of the civilian laborers. Dan Teters was the top boss over civilian construction on Wake Island and a very tough guy. The morning sun was shining brightly on the horizon when we passed Dan Teters house on our way to make the man-haul. Dan ran out of his house and flagged me down. One look and I knew that something was wrong.

Dan yelled that Pearl Harbor was being bombed by the Japanese at the moment. He ordered us to forget about our regular routines and report to Lieutenant Webb at the airport for further orders. I drove directly to the airport as fast as I could with Johnny.

Johnny and I were probably the first two civilians other than Dan Teters on Wake Island to know about the attack on Pearl Harbor. Since Wake Island was across the International Date Line, it was the morning of the eighth of December.

At first it was hard for me to believe what I was hearing, and I questioned the news report. Even after the report had been confirmed, it was still hard to accept. How could a small nation like Japan be so misguided as to think they could whip the United States? At that time I felt the United States was invincible. I said to Johnny, "Boy, are the Japanese ever going to be sorry for attacking Pearl Harbor."

"I am already sorry. We are sitting ducks on this sand pile," Johnny replied.

I had the most foreboding feeling that Johnny was right. Everyone was very aware that Wake Island was strategically located to Japan and we undoubtedly would be attacked. Suddenly the sharks' backbones were of little importance, and I dismissed the matter.

It was well past sunup when we found Lieutenant Webb. He ordered me to park the truck by the main tent where his office was located. After parking the truck, Johnny and I rushed into Lieutenant Webb's office and eagerly waited for orders. We were told that Lieutenant Webb would get to us as soon as possible.

Johnny and I patiently stood around Lieutenant Webb's office and waited and waited for orders. Since we were civilians, it was as if we did not count for anything and we felt ignored. I mentioned to Johnny we would get more attention if we were wooden store Indians. I do not think I ever felt so useless as I did while waiting for orders on that terrible December morning, destined to live forever in our history books as a day of infamy.

Military men were scurrying here and there, even pushing Johnny and me aside at times. I was beginning to think we had been forgotten in all the confusion and my mind began to wander. I was remembering the circumstances that brought me to Wake Island.

IT WAS A LITTLE OVER A YEAR ago towards the end of November 1940. I received a letter from Willis Dickerson. He was working at a sawmill in Applegate, California. He wrote there was a steady job for me if I would come. I was in desperate need for money and having steady work sounded too good to pass up, so I threw a few things in a bag and immediately drove there.

I was hired and started working right away. You had to work a month before you received your first check for the first two weeks. So if you quit or you were fired you always had two weeks' pay coming. By the time I had worked for a month without any pay, I was really hurting for money. When payday rolled around, the outfit announced it was broke and closed its doors. Nobody was ever paid. Needless to say, I felt like I had been used, and I had been. I was furious.

Willis felt terrible and apologized for ever telling me about that job. I did not blame him; it was not his fault. He was hurting for money just as much as I was. I could not think of anything profound to say, so I told him not to feel badly–that somehow things had a way of working out–and I told Willis goodbye.

Without any money, I had to return home to live with my parents and I was really depressed about that. It was not that my parents were not glad to have me, it was a matter of pride. As I drove I fussed and fumed about life's injustices.

I took the first job I could find. It was on a ranch in Kerby, Oregon. I met a fellow there who had worked for Nick Kurling, whose brother was one of the bosses for Morrison & Knudson, a large construction company located in Grants Pass, Oregon. He told me the company was hiring and paying good wages for men who would work overseas. Wages were still very poor for farm and ranch work, so my interest was immediately ignited.

I drove to Grants Pass as soon as I could and discovered that Morrison and Knudson had merged with other companies to form one large construction company called the "Big Five," to build defenses in the Pacific. Since I was blessed with the spirit of the wanderlust, it seemed like an answer to a prayer.

The Big Five consisted of Raymond Concrete Tile, Hawaiian Dredge, Morrison and Knudson, and J.H. Palmroy, all of which had merged with the Pacific Naval Air Base Construction Company.

The Big Five had government contracts to build air and naval bases on five islands, Wake, Guam, Midway, Cavite, and Palmyra for ten percent above cost to the contractors. I felt secure since the government was paying all costs, money would not be a problem. Time was the big concern. The government was anxious to have those bases finished as soon as possible.

They were to build not only an air base, but a submarine base on Wake Island. The giant company offered labor ninety dollars a month, laundry, room and board, all medical paid in full, plus a bonus of ten dollars every month until it reached one hundred twenty dollars. Then the money stayed at that amount as long as you remained working for them. After nine months I would get a thirty-day paid vacation and I could come home to the United States. If I returned after my vacation, the bonuses continued without being considered a break in service.

I filled out an application for the job of truck driver. I had a medical examination and I was accepted. A doctor gave me a series of shots for diseases I had never heard of. I was told that when I was issued a truck I would receive an additional thirty dollars a month. I was overflowing with happiness.

Like all young men of twenty-one, I saw that as the opportunity of a lifetime. I could satisfy my yen for adventure and see places I could only dream of while being paid good money. It was as if I had found the path that led to the pot of gold at the end of the rainbow. I drove home as quickly as possible to tell my dad and the family the wonderful news.

Until I had signed up with the Big Five, I had never heard of Wake Island. I scarcely had heard of Honolulu. I did not have the slightest idea where it was located. I found a world map and looked up Wake Island. After a careful search I was surprised to discover that Wake Island was no more than a tiny dark speck in the middle of a very large ocean. I determined it was about twenty-three hundred miles on the other side of Hawaii. It was closer to Japan than it was to Honolulu. And Midway was halfway between Wake Island and Honolulu.

A few of my closest friends were not very happy about my leaving for Wake Island. They reminded me that in the event of war, Wake could become a real hot spot. They did everything they could to talk me out of going there. I reminded them that I had already signed a contract. Besides, my brothers disagreed with my friends and urged me to go for the money. I was so blinded by monetary incentives and the lure of adventure I never gave a thought to asking myself, "If everything was so great, why were my brothers not going with me?"

I wavered just once. I was celebrating with a very good friend named Donna, who finally convinced me that going to Wake Island was a bad idea. I told her the only way to break that contract was to get myself thrown into jail for a crime. At least that is what I thought.

I started a fight in the tavern where we were partying. I threw bar stools out into the street and raised hell in general. The bartender refused to do anything about it. He liked me and did not want to see me get into any trouble. I could not even get thrown in jail when I wanted to. Once I was sober I was grateful to the bartender. I thanked him because I really wanted to go.

I knew if war broke out, Wake Island was a dangerous place, but the wages the Big Five offered was worth taking a chance for. You could not compare the money they were offering with the paltry sum of two dollars a day most ranch and farm workers were making in California. Plus they offered steady work with benefits. Even though work was getting more plentiful in the States than it had been in the past, things were still tough. You just could not find a job wherever or whenever you wanted.

Ever since Hitler had started to march across Europe, the government had been talking about war, yet nothing had happened. Even though I agreed it was a good idea to fortify the Pacific Islands, I never thought Japan would have the audacity to attack us. If we went to war I assumed it would be against Hitler. I never considered that as an immediate threat because Germany was so far away.

I lived in a world all my own and I never paid much attention to the real world's problems. It took all my industry just to survive through those lean years of the Great Depression. Getting that job on Wake Island changed my outlook on life. I had been so poor for so long I was convinced my future lay before me full of promise. I dreamed how well off I would be in just two years. I was going to be a man of substance; I was going to be wealthy.

Two weeks after being hired I received notice from the Big Five to come to San Francisco in four days. I would be leaving on the U.S.S. *Henderson.* I left my most precious possession with my dad for safekeeping. That was my 1934 Ford.

Before leaving, I celebrated with my kid brother, Skeet, and a friend named Joe. They really gave me a big send-off. I barely remember the trip to San Francisco. We partied hearty for days right up until the time I was to board ship. I was so intoxicated I could barely stand, and Skeet and Joe helped me to the entrance of the pier where uniformed guards stopped us. They were stationed at the entrance to keep all unauthorized personnel out. Skeet and Joe were not allowed to accompany me any farther. After showing my papers to the guards, they let me through the gate. I waved a final goodbye to Skeet and Joe. I was in such bad condition that without them to help me walk, I staggered to the ship, almost falling several times. I stumbled up the gangplank without fully realizing whether or not I was even on the right ship.

Once on board I wandered through the ship like a lost soul. I found what I thought was a good place to lie. It was on a tile floor, and I fell asleep. When I awakened I had the hangover of all hangovers. I was in the boiler room on the floor and the room must have been one hundred fifty degrees. I felt as if I was inside a sauna. I quickly made my way up to the outside. Considering the condition I was in, I do not understand how I found my way to that boiler room without someone stopping me. That was the first time I had ever been on a big ship, and I was in awe of everything around me.

The U.S.S *Henderson* was a transport ship that was far from the cruise ships of today's luxury liners. At that time I was told the navy only had two transports, the U.S.S. *Henderson* and the U.S.S. *Shaumont.* They were sister ships. Later during the war they made the *Henderson* a hospital ship.

Instead of heading to Hawaii, we sailed to Wilmington, California. That is where three hundred marines boarded. The ship was so crowded I slept up on deck. It was the stormy season and I was thankful that we never ran into any rough weather.

Despite any discomfort I might have experienced, I loved the open sea. I was one of the more fortunate who never experienced sea sickness, which enabled me to enjoy the ship's cuisine. All through the night and during the day, it seemed there was always someone hanging over the rail. After six days with nothing but ocean to look at, I thought maybe we were lost out there, although I did not care. The food was good and there was always plenty of good conversation.

When the ship docked at Honolulu, some of the men stayed aboard ship. However, many, including myself, were told we were to stay in a hotel for ten days before we boarded the *William Ward Burrows*, a freighter sailing for Wake Island. The *William Ward Burrows* and the U.S.S *Regulus* made steady runs to the islands being fortified, taking in supplies and men.

For ten days all my meals and accommodations at Honolulu were paid for by the Big Five. That left me with nothing to do but sightsee during the day and enjoy nightlife after dark. It seemed unbelievably perfect. It was as if I was on a paid vacation, and I enjoyed every minute of it. I could have probably become addicted to that easy fun-filled life had I not been so anxious to start building my financial future.

The *William Ward Burrows* was not nearly as crowded as the *Henderson.* I was assigned a bunk bed in a large room with several other men, but I still did not like the feeling of such an enclosed atmosphere as below deck. The air was stale and heavy at times with unpleasant odors. It was difficult getting a sound sleep with the irritating high and low notes of snorts and snores. So I stayed up on deck most of the time enjoying the fresh air of the open sea.

The freighter pulled three large barges about one hundred yards apart. They were loaded with heavy equipment and supplies of all kinds. The *William Ward Burrows* was a sea train of sorts.

I do not remember how many days it took to reach Wake Island. I just enjoyed the trip. When it was announced that we were there, I rushed to see the island that was to be my home. I could not see anything. It was not until we were practically on top of it before the island came into view. After all, it was only twelve and a half feet high. The islands were set in the shape of a horseshoe and not very wide. They could not have been over ten square miles, at best, from point to point.

Since there was not any docking facilities on Wake Island, the ship anchored about three hundred yards offshore. I was but one of many who were shuttled to shore in smaller landing crafts called lighters.

I was genuinely disappointed in the terrain. I was hoping for palm trees, sandy beaches, and lovely maidens. However, I found only hazardous coral beaches, small scrubby trees, thick bushy bushes that grew in abundance, and the only beautiful maidens were in my dreams. Nonetheless, I was so excited about work and making good money that nothing could dim my cheerful outlook on life.

My new home had been constructed for the civilian workers and was known as Camp Two. It consisted of over thirty large single-story barracks that housed approximately twelve hundred civilian workers. The camp was a small town in itself that had a commissary, administrative buildings, and warehouses. The camp had everything but women.

A large plant that made sea water into fresh water had been built on Wake Island for everyone's use. Without that facility there was no fresh water available.

It would be hardly worthwhile telling about my days of adjustment. I was looking forward to having a truck assigned to me but they were short on kitchen help, so I was assigned to the kitchen staff as a dishwasher. I worked with Larry Wah Bing Chinn and we became great friends. He called me Curly King because I had curly hair.

I had been working in the kitchen for three weeks when the Hawaiians and a few young men from Guam, who were the mess boys and waiters, rebelled. They did not make as much money as I did and they wanted a raise. Needless to say I was moved. I could not thank them enough.

I was finally given a gravel truck to drive. A few days later I was thrilled when a new green medium-sized International flatbed truck was assigned to me. From then on it seemed I spent most of my waking hours in that truck and, in time I swore that six-wheeled hunk of machinery had a personality all its own.

When I started my job as truck driver, I felt I had one of the best jobs on the island. I rode on a wave of self-satisfaction that I prayed would never end. I was to work nine hours a day, six days a week. Everything over eight hours was overtime, and I put in ten hours every day. I got as much overtime as I could. The money I received for overtime was more than my regular pay. My bank account was building rapidly.

Later, Johnny McCloud was assigned to help me. We were the island gophers so to speak. If we were not retrieving a needed part for the equipment or taking a work crew to the other side of the island, we were helping the cooks in the kitchen. Consequently I became acquainted with most everyone stationed there. Johnny and I liked being on our own and not having a boss watching our every move.

At first my daily life was a matter of simple routine. I was always up early and eagerly looked forward to every day. After breakfast Johnny and I would set up the benches that were built to fit on the flatbed of the truck and take the men to their work details. We called that a man-haul.

Then we would return to the mess hall and take down the benches. Next we loaded milk cans full of ice water and took them to the work crews. We would return to the mess hall and load several barrels of garbage and dump it on that side of the island known for the sudden drop-off into the ocean. Until lunch time we delivered whatever to whomever, wherever it was needed. Just before lunch we would set up the benches again to pick up the work crews and take them to the mess hall. After lunch our routine started all over again. After dinner my time was my own.

Since Johnny and I hauled garbage, we were told to watch out for the rats because they were as big as large cats and twice as vicious. If there were any rats I never saw a one. I believe the rats were exterminated long before I arrived and the fellows were just making conversation.

At first the days were long but I tried keeping busy so the time would pass more quickly. Still I had little to complain about. We were fed like lumberjacks. The men never wanted for anything when it came to food, although no matter how much I ate, I never weighed more than one hundred sixty-five pounds. I can truthfully say I never had it so good. Even my laundry was sent out to be washed and ironed.

With three hundred marines located on the other side of the island, about seven miles away, I felt quite safe. Their quarters were known as Camp One. Unlike our camp, they lived in tents that were set upon wooden platforms with wooden frames. The civilian camp was very much like army barracks, except inside we had thin wooden partitions opened at the top for ventilation and dividing the sleeping quarters. Having partitions to separate the rooms gave you the feeling of having your own space.

Two men were assigned to a room that was furnished with two built-in beds and two desklike dressers between the beds, which provided a minuscule feeling of privacy. Some men hung pictures of home, family, girlfriend, or movie stars on the wall, but I never felt the need to hang any pictures. The image of my dear ones were imbedded in my mind and were always with me. I did not have a closet. A foot locker served to store my things. The rooms had curtains for the doors. Since we were civilians we had our own mess hall, large ice houses, and a sub-station for electricity completely separate from the military facilities.

Under the circumstances I made myself as comfortable as possible and spent my time counting my money. Life held promise.

Chapter Two

IN MAY 1935 CONSTRUCTION BEGAN TO BUILD a seaplane base by Pan American airlines. Before the year ended the first Pan American airline clipper landed on the lagoon, thus inaugurating the Pan American "China Clipper" service. In 1937 Pan American started a hydroponics garden to grow food for their passengers. When I arrived in 1941 Pan American World Airways was well established with a small hotel and base on Peale Island to serve their clipper ships and passengers.

Unfortunately, there were no women on the island. Pan American hired only male employees. There was a civilian hospital on the other side of the island; however it was staffed by male nurses only. Many young men could not take the loneliness of living without women, so the turnover was tremendous. It seemed I was assigned a new roommate every other week. I would no more get acquainted to his habits and he would be gone. Then another would take his place and I would have to start all over again. Consequently I never became close buddies with them.

There was no social life to speak of either. The only entertainment was an outdoor theater that showed not-so-up-to date movies once a week. Church services were held on Sunday for those who wanted to attend. Some men played tennis, some played baseball, cards, or whatever they could dream up to help fill the lonely hours and pass the time. I played poker once in awhile with George Kelly for table stakes. Before I was assigned a truck I worked in the kitchen and I played penny ante poker with the cooks.

No one carried any large sums of money. If a man lost big he would have the paymaster deduct the amount from his wages and transfer it to whomever he owed. Most of the men had their checks put directly into a bank located in the United States. We carried vouchers or coupons that we could use to purchase items at the commissary. Those vouchers and coupons were deducted from our wages.

I was told the weather was usually very warm, so I brought mostly summer clothes. For that I was thankful because I found the summer temperature quite hot. Even when it was overcast, it was so humid I wore shorts. There were some chilly days during the rainy season. But even then I wore a slicker over the shorts to keep dry, and I would roast with that slicker on.

There was a few army personnel stationed on Wake and I was never quite sure why they were there. At first I thought they were part of the ground crew for the B-17s that landed to refuel on their way to the Phillippines. At that time the only air force the United States had was attached to the army and known as the Army Air Force. I discovered later they belonged to the Army Signal Corps and were a radio crew. There was also a few sailors on the island. Scuttlebutt was they were the crews for the navy's flying boats that were due to arrive any day to patrol the ocean for enemy activity.

Being a civilian it was difficult to keep straight who was in charge of the military. Of course I took orders from Dan Teters, and I do not believe he took orders from anyone. Commander Winfred S. Cunningham was the officer in charge of the naval activities and Wake Island. Major James P. S. Devereux was in charge of the marines. As civilians we were seldom told anything and had to rely on word of mouth.

Soon after the marines arrived their commander wanted to use a few of the civilian workers to build some very necessary defense installations such as bomb shelters, plane revetments, and gun emplacements. Our boss was very cooperative with the commander and agreed it was a good idea. Scuttlebutt around the camp was that the higher government and military officials who sat in their overstuffed chairs thousands of miles away thought better of it. They refused the marine commander's requests. Orders came down the chain of command that civilian workers were to do only what they were contracted to do. The marines had to build their own defenses. That decision later proved to be a disastrous one.

The marines armed themselves with picks and shovels to build the vital defense installations. That left little time for them to practice strategic drills of survival in case of attack. Since everyone on the island was in the same boat, so to speak, there was a friendly camaraderie between the civilian men and the military personnel. So in spite of what Johnny and I were told not to do, we helped the marines whenever possible, if we could do so without getting into trouble.

For example: We drove back and forth across the island many times everyday. When we passed marines working, we stopped whenever possible to ask if they needed anything from the other side of the island. We would bring whatever they wanted on our next trip. Such small considerations helped cement good relations.

There was a good library on the island. Up-to-date newspapers from the United States were available to keep us informed of everything happening back home. I read about the war in Europe and war talk in Washington was becoming old news. I ceased to worry about the dark clouds of war and being attacked on such a small island in the middle of nowhere.

There was construction in every direction that shouted trouble was on the horizon. Underground bunkers were built and camouflaged to store shiploads of ammunition being sent to Wake Island. I still did not worry. We had been warned so many times about the possibility of war that the warnings were like having sheduled fire drills every week. After awhile you paid little attention to them.

Even after the announcement was made that we could volunteer to learn how to use the .30 and .50 caliber machine guns, I did not worry. Some men were taught the proper procedure to follow when firing the big three and five-inch guns that were strategically placed around the island, and I still did not worry about war. I personally thought that activity was offered to help stem the turnover of men because target shooting became very popular with most of the civilan labor.

I presumed if the island were in immediate danger, we would certainly be sent more three-inch anti-aircraft guns and more up-to-date weapons instead of the old five-inch guns that had been taken from a World War I battleship. Little did I know that those guns were America's up-to-date weapons in the Pacific.

Johnny and I hauled sixty barrels of garbage away from the kitchen every day. After awhile I noticed several fish in that part of the ocean where we dumped the garbage. I began fishing on my off time. I discovered that the fishing was great. The more garbage, the larger the fish. It was not very long until the sharks arrived. From dumping the garbage every day at approximately the same time, I could look out over the ocean and watch several huge fins protruding out of the water announcing the arrival of sharks coming for their dinner. It was like watching a herd of cattle coming to the barn at feeding time.

The coral in the large lagoon had been dynamited to make a swimming pool for the men. To keep the sharks out of the swimming area, a strong fence had been built underwater. The men still became concerned about the number and size of sharks increasing every day. They could become a real threat if they ever broke or found a way through that fence. I was discussing the shark problem with a fellow, and he was the one who told me where to sell the sharks backbones in San Francisco.

I began making heavier fishing equipment. I will never forget the first big shark I hooked. I had a big piece of meat securely fixed to a large hook tied to a rope, which I had secured tightly around my waist. I never realized how powerful a shark was until that day. I had hooked a big one and was pulling him in when he suddenly took off out to sea pulling the rope so tight around me that I could not loosen it. I was jerked off my feet so hard that for just one or two seconds, I became airborne. When I hit the ground, I was dragged into the ocean. I panicked and no matter how much I tried, I was not able to free myself. I just knew I was a goner and the only land I would ever see again was at the bottom of the ocean. Suddenly the shark changed directions, loosening the rope, and I was finally able to free myself.

Then I worried about getting back to shore. I swam with all the strength I could muster and tried not to think of what might be right behind or underneath me. When I finally crawled upon the beach exhausted from the experience, I whispered a silent prayer of thankfulness to the Almighty for my deliverance. I was fortunate that day and learned a good lesson. Never tie a fishing rope to yourself, especially when fishing for something that weighs more than you.

When I caught a big shark I would cut his backbone out and bury it in the hot sand for a week. In that time the worms and other sand insects would have all the meat and cartilage eaten away, leaving only the bone. Once completely clean I would take it home. I planned to use iron wood for the cane handles since it was so plentiful on the island. The iron wood was from a small treelike bush very much like the Manzanita plant that grows in abundance in northern California.

Then came the day a dozen navy Grumman F4F-3 Wildcat fighter planes from the U.S.S. *Enterprise* landed on Wake. I was told they were staying as part of the defenses. That made me feel even more secure. Not only was I surrounded by America's finest marines, now the Navy Air Force was represented. I was too naive to see that my dreams of the future were in jeopardy and the good times were about to come to an end.

IT WAS JOHNNY WHO BROUGHT me back to reality when he disgustingly announced that we could grow old waiting for orders from the military. I shook my head in agreement because of the way Lieutenant Webb kept ignoring us. The thought crossed my mind that maybe we had become invisible. I told Johnny I felt as out of place as a donkey at the Kentucky Derby.

It was almost lunchtime. Johnny wanted to leave to get something to eat. We never had a chance to eat breakfast and we were hungry. I agreed with him and we turned to leave. That is when Lieutenant Webb finally called out to us. He ordered us to hurry over to camp one and get a barrel of oil for the big generator that ran the search lights at the airport. Now isn't that just like the military. After waiting for hours, Johnny and I were told to hurry.

There was a big water sack hanging close to where I had parked the truck and I stopped to get a drink. A young marine was standing there and motioned for me to go ahead of him saying, "I am not in any hurry. I have from now on."

I took a big drink and told the young marine thanks. I hurried to the truck and slid behind the wheel to drive. Johnny hopped into the truck on the other side and we were off. At last we felt like we were part of the action.

When the announcement was made that the Japanese were attacking Pearl Harbor, four Grumman Wildcats were immediately armed and sent out to fly patrol. Those planes returned later in the morning, and four other Grumman Wildcats continued the patrol.

The eight Grumman Wildcats left on the ground were quickly readied for war. The pilots were young and gung-ho. They took to the skies like hungry eagles and flew high, soaring overhead, searching for enemy prey, ready to attack anything that could be a threat. If need be, they were prepared and anxious to take on the entire Japanese Empire single-handedly.

After flying for hours and not seeing a thing and wanting to keep their planes ready for action, the pilots decided to land and have the planes serviced and refueled while they grabbed a bite to eat, since it was close to lunchtime. The pilots landed all eight Grumman Wildcats to be refueled at the same time.

Refueling the planes took time since there was only one small gas truck. The high-octane gas had to be transferred from large storage tanks into fifty-gallon barrels before taken to the planes and pumped by hand into the planes fuel tanks.

The eight Grumman Wildcats were coming in for a landing when Johnny and I left the airport. They were landing in pairs. Not side by side, but one a little offset from the other and a little behind. Johnny and I were returning with the oil and were about two-thirds of the way when I heard the unmistakable roar of several big planes. I looked over toward a low-hanging foggy type of cloud and I could just barely see them. The planes were coming in real low and heading straight for us. When they came into full view, I had the most foreboding feeling they were not ours. We only had twelve little fighter planes, and eight of them were landing when Johnny and I left the airport. I almost shoved my foot through the floorboard stopping that truck. I yelled for Johnny to jump out and hit the dirt. The planes flew directly over us, heading straight for the airport.

I am almost certain that Johnny and I were the first to see those planes coming in. As soon as we hit the ground, the first bomb exploded. Then another bunch of planes flew over and hit Camp Two. Then another wave hit the Pan American Hotel.

Johnny and I watched in horror as big plumes of dark smoke billowed high over the airport. When the attack ended the Japanese planes flew over us again and Johnny and I saw them waggle their wings in victory as they flew away. We jumped up and ran to the truck. We headed for the airport as fast as I could drive.

I believe that Johnny and I were first to get there with a truck. There was debris and devastation everywhere. The dead and the wounded were scattered all around. Men were yelling for help and screams of pain could be heard coming from every direction. It was as if we had driven into the bowels of Dante's *Inferno*. The air was heavy with smoke. So much so that my eyes hurt and it was hard to breathe. Johnny and I jumped from the truck to help the wounded.

Second Lieutenant Frank J. Holden, one of the pilots, had been riddled with bullets. George A. Graves made it to his plane only to be killed instantly when a direct hit burst his Wildcat into flames. Second Lieutenant Robert J. Conderman, another pilot, had almost made it to his plane when he was strafed. Being terribly wounded, he lay helplessly on the ground when a bomb hit his plane, pinning him underneath the wreckage. Despite every effort exercised in his behalf Lieutenant Conderman died later that night. Lieutenant Webb was down with bullets in his stomach and feet and after he was taken to the hospital. I never saw him again.

Seven of the eight fighter planes were on fire. The only plane not on fire was so shot full of holes it could not fly. There were twenty-five thousand gallons of high-octane gasoline, stored in a tank built upon cement stilts, burning so hot that the five hundred barrels of gasoline stacked behind it began exploding. The barrels blew unbelievably high into the air, creating quite an awesome spectacle. The fire was so hot it burned the hair on my arms from a block away. Nothing but devastation and death surrounded us.

Never had Johnny or I been faced with such an emergency, and we were at a loss how to handle those who needed immediate medical attention. We were not sure what we should do first other than help those who could not help themselves.

Someone yelled to pick up everyone who was down and get them to the hospital as quickly as possible. That order brought us to attention. Johnny and I quickly rolled that barrel of oil onto the ground and we began loading bodies on the truck. It was not for us to determine whether someone was dead or alive. If a man was down, we loaded him onto the truck. Johnny would pick them up by the arms and I would grab the legs to lift them on the truck. About that time several pickups showed up doing the same thing as we were.

I came across that young marine who told me to get a drink first–the one who said he had all the time in the world. He was lying face-up covered with dust. I became so emotional I could not touch him. Johnny checked him over and told me that he was dead. His time in all the world was not very long.

Johnny and I came to another young marine, and I reached down to grab his legs. One of his legs came off just below the knee and I almost fell over. I stood frozen and stared at the pieces I was holding, his foot and part of his leg were in my hand. I guess the shock was more than I could take because I became so sick I threw up.

15

So I could continue helping, I had to block out my emotions. I pulled myself together and I set my teeth determined not to become one of the casualties. I drove with Johnny as quickly as I could to the hospital. After unloading the men, we returned to get another load.

Earlier that morning a Pan American clipper had left for Guam. When Commander Cunningham learned of the attack on Pearl Harbor, he told the manager of Pan American airlines on Wake Island to have that clipper return at once. Upon returning, the huge clipper sat in the lagoon completely defenseless in the water. Like a big decoy, it could not have been more visible or more of an attractive target for the Japanese. With its large gas tanks filled, the clipper miraculously survived the onslaught of several strafes, only suffering twenty-three bullet holes. It was truly a wonder the clipper never caught fire and was able to fly without having any repairs. Although the clipper had survived, the Pan American hotel was completely destroyed during the first wave.

When the attack had finally ended and the last Japanese plane had disappeared from view, Pan American wanted to evacuate its employees as soon as possible. The pilots of the clipper threw out the mail and everything nonessential so they would have enough room for all their employees. That is everyone except the Hawaiians and the men from Guam, who worked in the kitchen. They were deemed as unimportant and left behind.

Two employees, Mr. Ramquist and Mr. Hevenor, missed the plane because they were elsewhere on the island helping the wounded. The pilots of the clipper were not about to wait for them to return. Mr. Ramquist and Mr. Hevenor ended up in a Japanese prison camp with us. The thought crossed my mind that should they survive the war they would never be late again for anything.

The clipper was so overloaded when it began taking off you could hear the motors struggling from any point on the island. It took three tries before the plane finally lifted away from the water. Once in the air, the clipper flew close to the water for the longest time and I wondered if they were going to make it. Little by little the clipper kept gaining altitude. I watched longingly until it flew out of sight. There was not a man on Wake Island who did not wish he was on that plane heading for Honolulu.

When the other four planes returned from patrol, the pilots were astonished to see all the destruction since they had not seen any enemy bombers. It was concluded the Japanese had taken advantage of the intermittent cloud cover that day and the patrol pilots missed seeing them. Although two of the pilots thought they spotted a formation, nonetheless, they were unsuccessful in catching them before the formation was lost in cloudy overcast.

There was so much to do that Johnny and I were kept busy every minute doing whatever we were told. After clearing the airport of all the wounded, Johnny and I were told to search through the brush that surrounded the airstrip for anyone who might have hidden there and was wounded or killed. Several of us combed the brush until it was determined there was no more dead or wounded to be found. While Johnny and I were waiting for further instructions, we heard that casualties were very light considering all the destruction and the number of men confined to such a small area.

Later, I heard the pilots had no more sat down to eat their lunch that day when planes were spotted in the distance. Someone shouted, "Do not be alarmed, those are the B-17's we are expecting." But instead, the planes were Japanese bombers.

I felt lucky I had been in between all intended targets that day. The barracks where I lived was strafed several times with machine guns. Thank God no one was inside at the time. Peale Island and the airport was heavily strafed. My truck must not have seemed important because the truck, Johnny, and I were left untouched. For that I was thankful.

There was not a man on the island who was not infuriated at the Japanese for their sneaky attack on Pearl Harbor and then on Wake Island. We were as united as any body of men had ever been since the beginning of time or probably would ever be again.

The island became a Mecca of activity. Everyone pulled together for defense. All nonessential construction ceased. The big bulldozers were put to work making the plane revetments that were so desperately needed for the four little stubby Wildcats we had left. More bomb shelters were dug. Large holes were excavated in which to hide the big vital equipment and covered over with netting in an effort to camouflage the machinery from enemy planes. Rifles and ammunition were issued to the civilians who had volunteered for combat duty. Many of the older civilians had been trained in World War I. Several other civilians volunteered to go to Peale Island and train to become a gun crew for a three inch anti-aircraft battery.

Men and boys from all walks of life were facing war for the first time. They were not trained for battle and did not know exactly what to do. In their effort to help that first day, they were falling over each other in the confusion. But it did not take long to get organized. Every man on the island had a job to do and we did it without question. With all efforts focused on defense projects, several were completed within a few hours.

Johnny and I took orders from everyone. We did not care. We just wanted to help in anyway we could. While at the airport I met Lieutenant Arthur A. Poindexter, who was ordered to cover the area around Camp One and the beaches there. He was busy putting together a detachment of men. I was ordered by another man in uniform to haul dynamite. The military wanted to lay dynamite around the airport to blow it up in case the Japanese landed.

The civilian dynamite house was located on Wilkes Island. Wilkes had been virtually untouched. Of course the marines fortified Wilkes with a gun battery, some three inch anti-aircraft guns and .30=and .50=caliber machine guns. Other than that there was nothing there but brush and birds.

By the time Johnny and I started out for the dynamite shed, the sun had disappeared over the horizon and darkness was rapidly enveloping the area. I had to get across that channel, and it took all the daring I could muster to drive onto that narrow little ferry in the dark. I knew better than to turn on any lights, so with Johnny guiding me I held my breath as I slowly drove onto the ferry. With just a few inches of leeway on each side, the picture of accidently having one wheel go over the side passed before my eyes and I would have to stop and make sure I was safely inside the margin of error. Once I was positive I had all four wheels on solid footing, I would slowly continue on. When at last I heard Johnny shout, "Okay, we made it," the relief I felt was enormous.

Johnny and I drove about a mile to the other side of the island to the dynamite house. With the help of two marines, we loaded that truck to capacity with boxes of dynamite. By then our eyes were becoming more accustomed to the darkness; yet, I still was not looking forward to crossing that channel again on that little ferry with the load I was carrying.

There was no place on that island where you could not hear the surf. With every unfamiliar sound we thought for sure the Japanese were landing. When Johnny and I began our trek back to the airport, I silently told myself to have courage even though I was scared through and through. I was so afraid I had completely forgotten how hungry I was. After all we had not had any food since the night before the attack. What I thought we needed at that time was a little levity, so in an effort to ease our troubled minds I reminded Johnny of our situation. There we were, just two civilians caught in the middle of a war without any weapons, with only a load of dynamite to hide behind. Johnny and I actually belly laughed over that, so much so I could hardly drive. For a moment we had escaped the gripping anguish of fear.

Chapter Three

THE FIRST STREAKS OF DAWN WAS ON THE HORIZON WHEN Johnny and I final-ly made it back to the airport. We were overly tired but dared not rest for fear of the consequences should any Japanese planes attack. Several men came to help us unload and I was thankful for that. After we finished, Johnny and I planned to grab a bite to eat, find cover, and capture an hour or two of sleep.

Before we could put our plan into action, Dan Teters arrived and ordered us to haul garbage from the kitchen for the last time. There would be no more meals served at the mess hall. Large gatherings were no longer allowed; from then on soup trucks would be set up and the men would have to eat where they could find a truck.

Dan Teters was taking over the responsibility of feeding the military. The civilian cooks were then fixing meals for everyone on Wake Island. That took a big load off Major Devereux's mind and left him more time to plan battle strategies. That also gave Lieutenant Poindexter the detachment of men he needed, which included the military cooks, office clerks, and a few sailors whom Commander Cunningham let him have.

Before we left, Dan Teters ordered us to report back for further instruc-tions as soon as we had finished hauling garbage. Just as we left the airport, I turned to see four of those stubby little Wildcats take off. I mumbled a silent prayer that they should have good hunting and return safely.

By that time Johnny and I were getting ravenous. We had not eaten since two nights ago and I felt weak. I told Johnny I had to find something to eat if I was to keep up our current pace. Johnny agreed and told me that he was getting shaky from lack of food and feeling strange from not having any sleep. I never thought I would ever live to see the day that sleep would be an inconvenience to survival.

The garbage barrels were located very close to the power house and the civilian ice house where the food that had to be refrigerated was stored. I no more stopped the truck to back up and load the barrels of garbage, than Johnny jumped out of the truck and told me to have Ohio help me load. He shouted he was going to dash over to the ice house and grab us something to eat. When I was backing up to load the garbage, I watched Johnny disappear into the ice house and the door closed behind him.

I never knew Ohio's proper name or why everyone just called him "Ohio". It was Ohio's job to separate the wet garbage from the dry, such as papers, and to burn everything that was burnable. Ohio and I were organizing the load when I heard planes. I looked up and saw a large formation of bombers flying very high overhead. I yelled at the top of my lungs for Johnny, and he could not hear me.

When the bombs began to fall, Ohio and I were caught out in the open without any cover whatsoever. I felt we were doomed and I silently whispered, "God help us." I started running toward the ice house and Ohio started running toward the lagoon. When I looked toward the lagoon, bombs were falling heavily there. I yelled for Ohio to stop and lie down, but I guess he could not hear me because of all the explosions. Ohio made it to the lagoon and jumped in. The lagoon was not very deep when the tide was out, and Ohio was running so fast he looked like a duck treading water on take off. I had no idea where Ohio thought he was going. So many bombs were falling into the lagoon it looked like it was raining.

I knew Ohio had panicked so I turned around and ran to catch him. I kept yelling for Ohio to lie down and he paid no attention to me. When I reached the lagoon I looked up and saw another bunch of bombs falling. I dropped into the water with a splat. As I fell I saw Ohio fall and I thought at last he had heard me. The bombs hit the water around us in several big explosions. As soon as Ohio thought the planes had passed over us, he jumped up and began running again. I yelled for him to stay down. Planes were still overhead and more bombs were being dropped. I swam under water as deep as I could get. I could hear the bits of shrapnel splatter across the water missing me completely.

When I felt the worst of the bombing was over, I looked around to locate Ohio. He was not so lucky. The water was pinkish red with his blood and at first I was afraid for Ohio. I made my way through the water to reach him as fast as possible. I saw he had been hit in the shoulder, and I breathed a sigh of relief that he was still alive. Ohio tried to get up and fell. I told him to stay down until I could help him. After a quick examination of the wound, I felt it was not very serious since the bleeding had stopped. I told Ohio he would be all right and we stayed lying in shallow water until the attack was over.

The bombing only lasted a few minutes. When I tried to help Ohio stand he yelled, "Put my clothes out! They are on fire."

"No they are not. Come on and I will take you to the hospital. You are going to be all right," I reassured him again. I helped him up and supported him as he staggered half dazed to the truck. Until then I had been looking away from the hospital. When I looked toward the hospital, I saw it was on fire along with several barracks and the big warehouses.

Ohio and I were standing next to the truck, dripping wet, when Johnny came out of the ice house stuffing his face. He had a big salami under one arm and a large cheese roll under the other. He looked around and saw all the fires and smoke across the lagoon and shouted, "What in the hell happened?"

"Ohio and I were almost killed. That is what happened. We were bombed again."

"I thought I heard something, but I was too hungry to give a damn," Johnny said.

I just shook my head and laughed to think that Johnny was stuffing his face while death and destruction were falling all around him. I told Ohio that Johnny must have an angel sitting on his shoulder.

Johnny and I helped Ohio into the truck. I drove as fast as I dared to find a doctor while Johnny held onto Ohio to keep him from falling in case he passed out. He had a hole in his shoulder about four inches long and two inches wide. The wound was in the middle of his shoulder blade. It was not a bullet hole like I thought, but a piece of shrapnel imbedded deep inside his shoulder.

After every raid there was a certain amount of confusion between the military and the civilians being given new assignments. After hurrying to find a doctor in the midst of all the devastation, Ohio was told to come back later. There were too many other men who were more seriously wounded and needed immediate attention. Doctor Kahn poured iodine over Ohio's wound and told him it was not life threatening and he would remove it the following day. We left Ohio in the care of the medical staff.

That day the Japanese bombers concentrated all their efforts on Peale Island, destroying the machine shop, warehouses, administrative buildings, and worst of all, the hospital, even though large red crosses had been painted all over it. Bombing the hospital only filled us with more anger and resolve.

When I thought about all those helpless young men I had taken to the hospital the day before only to be killed a day later. I wondered where God was in their hour of need. It was enough to try one's faith.

There were four ammunition magazines located on Wake Island. Two were chosen to be the new hospital quarters since each had its own generator. Doctor Lawton E. Shank was the contractors' doctor. He was a civilian and took over one, while Gustave M. Kahn, a lieutenant in the Medical Corps, took over the other. Civilians and marines worked side-by-side into the night moving out the ammunition and bringing in beds and medical supplies. Another magazine was implemented to serve as the new radio facility since the communication center had been destroyed.

Thanks to Johnny, my stomach was at last satisfied. I was so hungry I literally inhaled every bite of salami and cheese as I drove to the airport for further instructions. Johnny and I did not leave so much as a crumb to fall by the wayside. We were not sure when we might get to eat again.

When we arrived at the airport, Johnny and I were told that the airport's one and only gasoline truck had been caught out on the airstrip and had been destroyed in that second bombing. The driver had two marines riding with him and he did some fancy driving trying to escape the falling bombs, but a direct hit blew up the truck, killing all three instantly.

Once again Johnny and I had escaped a Japanese onslaught of planes without a scratch, and for that I was thankful. I was beginning to think we led a charmed life. Even the truck I drove was untouched.

By then Johnny and I were beginning to move like zombies, forgetting what we were supposed to do next. That is when I remembered Dan Teters's orders to haul garbage. If nothing else, Johnny and I were dedicated. We returned and loaded barrels of garbage, then drove to that part of the island to empty them into the ocean. It seemed a little silly to worry about the trash when there was so much destruction around us that needed attention.

Johnny and I were told all efforts were in motion to protect the freshwater plant. We were ordered to pick up as many fifty-gallon barrels as we could find. Those barrels were to be filled with fresh water and stored about the island. Since the barrels had been filled with gasoline at some time or other the water would undoubtedly taste terrible. Regardless, the water would be drinkable and would be much better than going thirsty. The civilians took over the job of filling and setting those barrels around the island.

After the water barrels were filled and set from one end of Wake Island to the other, Johnny and I debated whether to sneak away and grab a wink or two or return to the airport for further orders. We were exhausted. I decided I could go no farther and I pulled to the side of the road and stopped. Just to close my eyes for a few minutes felt so satisfying I wanted to sleep and forget about everything in general. However, my conscience would not allow me that luxury. When I thought about our situation, I felt so guilty I could not sleep. By resting we were letting our team down. Johnny was restless, too, and having trouble sleeping. He confessed he felt the same way as I did, so we returned to Dan Teters for more orders.

The food warehouses had been destroyed, so Johnny and I were ordered to load what boxes of food supplies were still intact and scatter them across the island, too. Hundreds of civilians joined us in that effort. We buried cases of canned meats, vegetables, fruits, and beans from one end of the island to the other. If you were hungry and could not make it to a gun emplacement, you just dug up a crate of food and ate whatever was there. Just about everyone had extra food hidden around their foxholes. No one I knew ever went hungry. We had as much food buried as we did ammunition. Nevertheless, in the days to come it became a real treat to just get a single slice of freshly baked bread.

While Johnny and I were busy burying cases of food, other civilians were taken to Wilkes Island to fill sandbags for the gun emplacements. Other civilians volunteered to set up a new camp at Peacock Point so they could stay close to help with the gun battery located there.

First Lieutenant John F. Kinney and Sergeant William J. Hamilton, with the help of a few airmen and mechanics who had survived that first attack, began immediately salvaging what they could from the seven destroyed planes. They scavenged enough tools and parts to do minor repairs on the planes. But with the ingenuity that Americans are known for, they performed miracles. They kept those little pot-bellied Wildcats flying. They fixed the one Grumman Wildcat that had not burned in that first raid. Like the fabled Phoenix, so did one Grumman Wildcat rise from twisted metal.

I believed it was just a matter of time before reinforcements arrived, and I wondered how the Big Five was going to figure my over time. I had a month's paid vacation coming and a trip home I was looking forward to.

After the second bombing, foods were simplified even more to one-dish meals such as stews, soups, or sandwiches. Huge cooking kettles were set up outside in the open air. New plans were made for meal distribution. The food was going to be taken to the gun emplacements and several points about the island every morning and night. It was up to the men to get there if they wanted to eat.

Eventhough meals had been simplified, Johnny and I still had to haul garbage, men still had to be driven to their appointed tasks, oil, gas, and ammunition still had to be hauled and equipment taken to where it was needed. Johnny and I were still island gophers.

That was my first taste of war. Those first two days were so hectic that self preservation was not even a priority. We were kept so busy we did not take the time to sleep or eat. Like the military, Johnny and I were reduced to short naps. Everyone drove themselves to the limits of endurance. We were all red-eyed and exhausted from lack of rest. We were all determined to show Japan it would have to pay a heavy price for attacking Wake Island.

Having that truck to drive allowed me more freedom of choice about everything. When things began to calm and there was more organization, my thoughts turned to self-protection. Nobody with any sense stayed in the barracks anymore. Everyone had grabbed a shovel and took to the bushes to dig a foxhole to sleep in.

I drove to the barracks with Johnny and we grabbed pillows, blankets, and anything else we thought we could use. We threw everything on the truck bed and I drove away from all machinery and buildings. Johnny and I dug a large foxhole that would hold the two of us. I never parked the truck close to our foxhole. I was not taking any chances of becoming a casualty and miss going home for the holidays.

It was not long until more civilian men looking for cover joined us and we became eight, so we dug a bigger hole. When we finished we had a big underground room for sleeping. We scavenged scrap lumber to support a camouflaged roof of dirt and brush. Even though we had suffered losing the convenience of buildings, we made the best of it.

Most civilians wanted to fight, but as civilians we did not have any weapons. Some of the older men who had not been issued guns after the first attack gathered what guns they could confiscate as the fatalities mounted. Those who did not have any weapons gave their total moral support and helped wherever and whenever there was a need. A few military men did not understand that we needed moral lifting, too, as part of a team. Our spirits were lifted every time we heard our side had shot down a Japanese plane or sunk one of their ships.

There was little rest for us at night. We usually went to sleep at dawn and slept until the Japanese bombers came. It was during those periods of rest my mind would wander to home, family, and what used to be. I would think about my childhood. I could not help but wonder if I would ever see my family again.

I WAS FOURTH OF SEVEN children. My dad's name was Richard Columbus King and everyone called him Dick. My mother's name was Elizabeth and everyone called her Bessie. Like all large families of that era, they worked very hard for very little.

In 1924 my grandfather died, leaving my dad three hundred acres located in Stonewall County, Texas. Dad sold the ranch where we lived in New Mexico to his brother, Jim King. He already owned the farm next to ours, so he was happy to buy it, and we moved to Texas.

For the next three years we lived the good life in Texas. Dad even gave five acres to a church to bring the Holy Word closer to us. Then in 1927 Coley caught rubeola, otherwise known as German measles. Within a short time the whole family became sick with severe colds and high fevers. Mother confined all of us to bed.

Mother worked almost twenty-four hours a day in loving yet rigorous care keeping us fed and doctored mostly with home cures. We lived quite a ways from town, and in those days you had to be near death before you ever went for a doctor. We never had a telephone, and all too often by the time a doctor got to you, it was too late.

To treat colds and congestion, Mother would wrap her finger in a soft cotton rag and dip it in coal-oil. She then swabbed our throats out with it. She mixed turpentine, coal-oil and Vicks together and rubbed it on our chests. She made us pull the covers up and breathe the fumes deeply into our lungs. Dad helped Mother as much as he could. Unfortunately, he never realized just how sick she really was, since Mother was not a complainer.

My mother and three-month-old brother caught German measles. Mother was nursing the baby when she became ill. After taking care of everyone else, there was nobody well enough to take care of her. The family chain was broken when Mother and the baby developed pneumonia and both died within hours of each other. Losing my mother was the saddest day of my childhood. My mother and baby brother were buried together in the same coffin at the Double Mountain Cemetery in Peacock, Texas.

I knew about death, but I never had to acknowledged the finality of it before. I had watched Dad kill chickens for us to eat or slaughter a steer. I had even found the stiff body of a bird or come across a dead animal when riding a horse around the ranch. Still, I never gave death a second thought. But losing my mother was the first really true comprehension of death, its conclusion, and the sorrow I felt in relation to someone I loved.

Without my mother's loving and spiritual influence, there was a definite void in the home. Things started going downhill rapidly. There was not very many bright spots in our otherwise drab existence and the family would never be the same again.

With so many children, Dad had more responsibility than he could handle alone, and within a short time he married a seventeen-year-old girl named Iva Francis Webb. She was the daughter of a neighbor of ours. Iva looked very much like Mother in every way.

Dad remarrying never upset me or my younger brother, Skeet, or my little sister Syble, like it did my older brothers, Coley and Red. My older sister Velma was fifteen then and not too happy about the situation, either.

Iva was only two years older than Velma and awkwardly more like a playmate than the unwanted disciplinarian we were forced to be nice to. They never fully accepted Iva as their mother even though Iva expended every effort to bring up the children. It would be years later and eight more children before Iva gained the respect of the family as being our father's wife.

Dad sold the two-hundred-ninety-five-acre farm, and we moved into town where I began school. Dad had taken a restaurant as down payment on the farm and the balance on credit. About that time the Great Depression started. There were no jobs and nobody had any money. Things kept getting worse and just when we thought they could not get any worse, they did. The restaurant did not do very well and the banks failed. Dad was never paid for his land and he lost everything.

Dad struggled for many years trying to get another foothold in life. Iva began having children of her own almost immediately, and our already-impoverished family started growing in number.

Being a rancher, Dad could not find a steady job and he was forced to work part-time at whatever he could find. With Dad and our new stepmother, we moved hither and yon, back and forth across Texas. Dad was always on the lookout for whatever work he could find to care for his large brood.

At that time in my young life, I thought I knew all about death and the unhappiness one feels when losing a loved one. Because of the insecurity of life I experienced, I had unhappy dreams and I would be brought to fully awake by mixed emotions. I still missed mother and sometimes I felt badly that she let death take her. I told myself that I would spit in the grim reaper's eye before I gave up my life. With those naive thoughts I would roll over and fall back into a restless sleep.

I WOULD BE ABRUPTLY AWAKENED by the frightening sound of heavy bombers overhead. Frightening because *of* the death and destruction we suffered after every bombing. As soon as the bombs stopped falling, Johnny and I would jump up, run out to the truck, and start hauling men and supplies to wherever needed. We helped the marines move the gun emplacements at night. In fact I spent most *of* the night, every night moving guns.

Like sand crabs we crawled out of our holes and worked through the night preparing for the following day's assault. We became masters at disguising the guns. We used stove pipe or anything we could find to make phoney guns. The observation planes that flew over regularly during the day and took pictures were fooled by those deceptions.

On the third day the Japanese concentrated their bombing where they thought the gun positions were. The Japanese headed straight for Battery E. They blew up the wooden gun that we had installed the night before. Thank goodness we had moved that big five-inch gun. The Japanese planes made passes over the other gun emplacements, but we were lucky. They missed every target. Slight damage was done to Camp One, but not one big gun was lost. Over all there was little destruction for all the bombs they dropped that day.

The big gun battery on Wilkes Island looked impressive, but that gun did not have any sights. It was supposed to be used for the defense of the beaches. That was the gun that several civilians went over to help a few sailors man. If they hit anything in the air, it was by pure luck.

Unfortunately, the Japanese got lucky when they hit the shed that housed the civilian dynamite on Wilkes Island. Those explosions were the most spectacular I had ever seen, so large they damaged two of our big guns. The brush caught fire and the birds that survived flew wildly about the islands. The landscape looked like there had been a pyroclastic flow from a volcano's eruption. When the explosions finally came to an end there was not any brush, birds, or anything left on Wilkes Island.

I was told Captain Elrod shot down a Japanese bomber before it reached Wake Island that day. We gave him a big cheer of thanks. At least that would be one less bomber we had to worry about the next day. The guns that were damaged were quickly repaired. That night we moved Battery E again, and a dummy gun was made to replace the real one.

It is a wonder I did not forever have a kink in my neck from always looking up. Even though the raids always came approximately the same time everyday, I always expected the unexpected. Even if we made mistakes, the Japanese made bigger ones. Many of their bombs missed the island completely. Even the big guns on the Japanese warships shot shells that whizzed over us and fell into the ocean. The men would break out laughing making jokes about our enemy's eyesight. Making jokes about the Japanese was the only way we had of keeping our morale up. However, the echos of laughter was to be the death knell for life on Wake Island as we knew it.

Chapter Four

ALTHOUGH WE WERE ALWAYS BEING TOLD BY DAN TETERS that help was on the way, there was not a man on the island who I knew that was not scared through and through. Most of us learned to live with fear and control it, but a few could not. I felt very sorry for them.

I will never forget one man who I will call Al. I would not want to embarrass his family by telling his real name. Al came to share our foxhole and we gladly took him in. At that time we did not realize how much mental help he needed and what a big problem he would become. Al never came out of shock after the first raid and he would not leave that underground room. He lay in his own body fluids and fecal matter until the room smelled so bad we could not take it. We finally were so desperate we literally dragged Al to the lagoon and threw him in. We told him to wash himself and his clothes before coming out, or we would not let him back into the dugout with us.

The shock of us throwing him into the lagoon brought Al to reality. After that, Al left our underground room to relieve himself but only then. Al would be one of the men who stayed on Wake Island as a prisoner of war. As we know from our history books, Rear Admiral Shigematsu Sakaibara was the Japanese commander of Wake Island who ordered the execution of all prisoners of war there in October 1943. For that offense he was hanged as a war criminal after the war.

By the fourth day I began to wonder when the cavalry was going to arrive. We were told by the military and Dan Teters that help was on the way and to keep a stiff upper lip. Just hearing that bit of good news restored the morale and lifted the troubled spirits of the men for a couple of days. Then after two or three days, when nothing appeared on the horizon, Dan Teters would tell us that again. He was excellent at managing men skillfully.

After every pep session I would repeat, "Boy those Japanese are going to get it a hundred times over for picking on us." I really believed what I was being told, and I would continue doing whatever was necessary to help the marines halt the Japanese onslaught. Being civilians, the military never let us know just how desperate things really were.

The large ice boxes at Camp Two were still intact. Since I drove a flatbed truck, Johnny and I were ordered to haul the dead there everyday to be stored until a proper funeral could be given them. It was the only way we had of storing our deceased until help arrived. It was disheartening to see my comrades being stacked like cordwood inside those ice boxes.

That night we had no more finished moving the guns when ships were discovered south of the island. The marines told us to expect landing parties anytime. Johnny and I were really scared when we heard that. Neither of us had ever had any hand-to-hand combat training so we beat it back to our dugout. Nobody in our little group had any weapons and everyone was afraid of what we might have to face tomorrow. We tried staying calm by sharing stories of happier times.

With the coming of daylight the sound of man-made thunder filled the air. Explosions seemed to come from every direction and we knew they were not ours. Several big shells whizzed overhead, exploding in the ocean. There was nothing any of us could do but pray in silence and wait for company to arrive.

There were so many explosions and Wake Island was so small I could not help but wonder if the island might sink. After two hours of constant shelling I wondered why our five-inch guns were not shooting back. I felt like a rat in a trap.

I did not know that Major Devereux had ordered a cease-fire until the Japanese ships came well into range. The Japanese ships were equipped with bigger and longer range guns than we had. By holding fire, Major Devereux lured them in so close that when our big guns did open up, the Japanese suffered heavy losses before they could escape.

Finally the sound of the five-inch guns being fired filled the air and that was so satisfying to my ears. As long as I could hear those guns booming across the island, I knew there was still hope of being rescued, and a chance to see tomorrow. It was like having a reprieve from an unknown fate that surely would end in death.

There was so much shelling I could not stand not knowing what was happening. I stuck my head out to see and I saw one hell of a battle going on. The air was heavy with the smell of gunpowder.

"Can you see anything?" someone yelled. "What is going on out there?" another shouted.

"I cannot see much through all the smoke, but our side is holding," I replied. I looked over toward the truck. Even though it was covered with a heavy dusting, you could see that green paint in the sunlight. That truck was always in the open and made a good target for the Japanese since I never took any time trying to camouflage it. It was an inviting mark for the Japanese to shoot at, yet it never sustained a scratch.

I realized there was nothing I could do at the moment, so I backed down into the shelter and waited for the shelling to cease. I knew there would be plenty to do then. I felt so useless while waiting. I silently prayed that all the firing I heard coming from out at sea was the big guns of the U.S. Navy. All of us were unaware of the devastating blow the navy suffered at Pearl Harbor.

There were so many explosions the rats I never saw before came out. Two crawled into the dugout with us. We stomped and hit them with anything at hand. Those rats never had a chance and we showed them no mercy.

The shelling continued on and on. After the excitement of having a rat invasion, everything calmed inside our dugout. I was too exhausted to worry anymore about the present. I saw a chance to capture some rest. I had not had a good sleep since the war started. I leaned back against the dirt wall and fell into a profound sleep. I slept amidst the thundering sound of war going on around me. Once in awhile I felt the ground shake under me from the reverberations of the bombs exploding nearby, and I would open my eyes to check on everything. Once I saw everyone was all right, I closed my eyes and fell into nothingness again. If a big shell was meant to explode near enough to kill me, I did not want to hear it coming.

My subconscious began to dream. My dream wandered to the life I had lived as a young boy, a life filled with hard times, good times, and a freedom I would probably never experience again.

MY DREAM VIVIDLY PORTRAYED THE first place we had moved after Dad had lost everything. It was called the Allen place near the Double Mountains out of Peacock, Texas. I had to walk three miles to a country school. Many times I would have to go without lunch because the family did not have enough food. And more times than I remember we had only beans for supper or just potatoes.

I never knew we lived in extreme poverty and were considered poor because everyone around us lived in the same environment. Having hardships was just part of living. Nobody had any money and everyone had problems during those dark days of the Depression. No matter how poor you were you walked with your head held high.

I never lived in a house that had anything but the uncomfortable outhouse, decorated with the unmistakable moon on the door and a catalog inside for reading and other necessary needs. Making that chilly trek in the middle of the night was a way of life. I also never lived in a house that had running water or electricity. We always had to pump our water by hand and use kerosene lamps at night.

With all those negatives you might think we were miserable. On the contrary, we had a wonderful, close, and loving relationship within the family. We always had a birthday cake on our birthdays. The cake may have not been decorated with any frosting, but we always had a cake and a little celebration to make our birthday special. And most of all we were happy.

We moved again to what was known as the Gilt ranch in King County, Texas. My stepmother was pregnant again and Dad was at his wits' end. We did not have any money and Dad decided we could not stay there, either, so we moved in with a relative of ours. Needless to say that did not last very long, and we moved back to Peacock, Texas.

What woeful remembrances I had of those early years. I had to get up before daylight to do chores during the winter, and it was cold. I had to walk two miles down a washboard road to catch the school bus, then ride thirty miles across barren land to reach school. By the time I returned home and finished my evening chores, it made a considerably long hard day for me.

Skeet was two years younger than me. His given name was David Russell King. I never knew why everyone called my younger brother Skeet. We just did. My brother Coley was two years older. His given name was Richard Columbus King, after Dad. Since it was confusing for both of them to have the same name, the family nicknamed him Coley.

We were not at Peacock very long, either. Dad threw his hands up and declared he was taking the family back to New Mexico. Back to the land and the people whom he knew so well, back to the same area where he had lived years before. I can truly say I was overjoyed when we moved away from Peacock, Texas.

My oldest sister, Velma, and my oldest brother, Red, stayed in Texas. Velma had a good job at the Stonewall county office and she was not about to give it up. Red, on the other hand, was born a hundred years too late. He was what you would call a saddle tramp, a drifter of sorts. His best friend and his only true love was his horse. Red's given name Julius Gilbert King. Since he was the only one in the family who had red hair everyone called him Red. He was six years my senior.

It was like a miracle to me when we returned to the same house where I had lived with my birth mother, the very place Dad had sold to his brother Jim when we moved to Texas. Because we were so desperate my uncle Jim let us live there for nothing. It seemed like a lifetime had passed since I lived there during those happy days with Mother. It was like I had lived in another world then even though only four years had passed.

The house was not nearly as big as I remembered. The wallpaper was faded and torn in every room. The house echoed of bygone days, and my heart saddened that we had returned under such unfortunate circumstances. The house had only two bedrooms. Dad, Iva, and the baby took one; all the rest of us took the other. Although it was crowded, the sound of laughter could always be heard between us.

Dad was sure he could find a steady job as a ranch-hand on one of the larger ranches nearby, and he finally found steady work on the Calumet ranch east of Dexter, New Mexico. It was a big ranch and we moved into a house located on the ranch. By then it was the beginning of 1932. I began school again.

I can honestly say for the next three years I hated the winters with a passion of pure dread. They were brutal. It was flat country and icy winds seemed to blow constantly. I had four miles to walk to school.

The country was still plagued with economic ills that seemed unsolvable. It was into the second year at the Calumet ranch when President Franklin D. Roosevelt ordered or had a law passed to destroy a certain percentage of the livestock, including cattle, sheep, hogs, etc. For killing the cattle, the government paid the Calumet ranch twelve dollars a head. I do not know how much was paid for the other animals. That was done to restore the economy of the country.

Dad and a few cowboys rounded up three hundred head of cattle and drove them to a deserted area on the high plains and shot them. The pitiful part of the story was there were hungry people in the big cities. Soup lines had been set up by the government to feed the multitudes. Yet the ranch was not allowed to give a single steer to the poor. I have never been able to understand that kind of waste, that kind of logic.

While living at the Calumet ranch I watched the same herd of wild horses come to the ranch for water every day. Then one day a handsome, strongly masculine stranger rode up on a big sorrel gelding. I can still picture him in my mind. He was tall in the saddle, wore a big black hat, leather chaps, and Chihuahua spurs. He had the nicest grin like he had a secret that he was not telling you. He was just about the fanciest cowboy I had ever seen.

He told us his name was Dallas and he needed a place to stay for the night. Dad graciously told him he could stay with us. Dallas talked real slow. Iva told Dad if a rattlesnake was under Dallas's chair it would bite him and he would die before he could tell you about it. The next morning Dallas told us thank you for our hospitality and said goodbye. After Dallas left we never saw that herd of wild horses again. A week later we heard Dallas was in jail for stealing them. Later Dallas was acquitted when the horses were recovered.

About that same time while on vacation, Velma came to visit us. Velma visited Dallas at the jail and fell in love. Velma and Dallas were married soon after that and Velma never returned to Texas.

I was still living at the ranch when I finished the seventh grade. I do not know why Dad quit his job at the Calumet ranch since everything was so uncertain in those days. But he did and we moved close to Hagerman, New Mexico, back to the area where I was born.

I had been given a horse named Cherry and I worried that Dad might not let me keep him. I loved that horse. Cherry was the first animal I ever had that was all mine. I rode him at every opportunity. I had worried for nothing because when we moved, Dad took Cherry with us.

Dad secured a job on the Buffalo Valley farm and we moved into a house that was located on the farm. In the three years Dad had worked for the Calumet farms he had accumulated fifty head of cattle. Dad sold them and for awhile that gave us a little money to live on. However, it seemed no matter how hard Dad worked, things just did not work out for him. There were times when Dad had to kill a stray steer to keep his large family from going hungry, and it was not always his steer, although he tried not to make a habit of it.

About that time Coley quit school and left home to try it on his own. I looked up to Coley and knew I was going miss him terribly. Secretly I wanted to go with him. Skeet was then the only brother left at home whom I felt close to. He looked up to me the way I looked up to Coley and that made me feel very important. I was going to school for the last time ever. By then I had two half-brothers, Billike and Frank, and one half-sister, Nina Mae.

I was entertaining the idea of leaving home to be on my own. I considered myself grown up. At the time it seemed more important to do what I wanted and attending school was not a priority. I also felt Dad already had more than he could take care of. I reasoned that if I were not there, at least Dad would have one less mouth to feed. I could not leave without Dad's consent, so I kept quiet until I felt I had a chance.

WHEN THE SHELLING STOPPED I awakened and it seemed as if days had gone by. For a moment all track of time was lost. However, it took only a few seconds to fully recover my senses and realize where I was.

Johnny and I quickly loaded the truck with civilians who wanted to help, then drove everyone to the airport to receive orders. We were ecstatic to discover the marines had run off the Japanese landing party, shot some Japanese bombers out of the sky, and the big guns had sunk a couple of ships. Hearing all that made us feel pretty good. We could not wait to spread the good news to the other civilian men.

The little Wildcats had quite a day, too, but not without taking a toll on the planes. Major Paul A. Putman and Captain Frank C. Tharin's planes suffered many bullet holes. When they were able to land safely, the planes were refueled as quickly as possible. Lieutenant John F. Kinney and Lieutenant Carl R. Davidson took over. They too had a very big day with the credit of shooting down two bombers and heavily damaging a third. Captain Herbert C. Freuler had his oil line shot through and had to land. The motor was ruined and could not be repaired. Captain Henry T. Elrod had to make a crash landing and his plane was totaled. Our small air force consisted of only two airplanes plus another that had been patched together.

The big navy ice boxes were filled with our dead and there was no more room for the latest casualties. Johnny and I wore told to take the truck and help haul the bodies from the navy ice boxes and help bury them in a large mass grave that was being dug at that very moment. I made no objection, although I had mixed feelings of dread. I had taken many bodies there and I knew what to expect; I knew what was waiting for me. A knot formed in my stomach as the feeling of hopelessness came over me, because I knew with that order the end was near if help did not arrive soon.

There were several men already there when I arrived. The bodies had frozen together and I helped pry them apart with a tire iron. That was the most distasteful task I have ever had to do. How I kept from crying I do not know, because I felt sad and sick inside having to handle my comrades in such a heavy handed, heart wrenching, and unorthodox way. It was almost more than I could endure. The bodies were loaded onto my truck and I drove them to a large trench that had been specially prepared for a mass grave. That task will always be branded in my memory as one of the worst things I had ever had to do in my life.

After the burial, a short prayer was said and marines fired a last salute. Commander Cunningham, Major Devereux, and Dan Teters was there to witness and pay their last respects. Commander Cunningham issued new orders. He told everyone from then on the dead would be buried where they fell.

The big guns had to be moved again and it took one hundred civilians to help move Battery D at Toki Point to the other end of Peale Island. We barely finished getting the new gun emplacement set when dawn was breaking over the horizon. We dashed to our dugout to grab some rest before the next raid.

The Japanese changed their schedule and the next raid came early. However, little damage was done. After every bombing it was the same routine for Johnny and me. We helped with the dead and wounded and hauled food and water or ammunition. There was always something to do. When it was time for us to return to the dugout, we played cards, reminisced about the past, and talked about things in general. We never talked very much about the future, only about what might happen tomorrow. We lived one day at a time. I felt that every day was a miracle when I was still alive at the end of it. Every day I would look to the horizon for help to arrive. Nothing ever appeared except more Japanese warships, and my morale would sink ever lower.

That is when Major Devereux would get out his soap box and give everyone another pep talk reassuring us that help was coming in seventy-two hours. The pep talks did serve a purpose. They made everyone feel better for a little while. In the light of our desperate situation and considering the only other alternatives left to us, I wanted to believe Major Devereux. The thought of surrender was not an option at that point. Even without the pep talks I was so mad at the Japanese for their sneaky attack and for ruining my plans for the future, I was filled with determination to endure to see them beg for forgiveness. And I would do whatever was necessary to help the marines halt the Japanese onslaught. Even though the marines had fought courageously, it was another miracle that they were still holding.

All was quiet on the sixth day; it seemed almost too good to be true. Although I enjoyed having a chance to relax it was like waiting for the other shoe to drop and I was filled with apprehension. Some men took advantage of the lull to finally get some much-needed sleep, some went for a swim in the lagoon to clean up. And some worked on defenses. In spite of any negative feelings I may have had, all of us enjoyed having a quiet day.

There was a great deal of speculation between us wondering what the enemy was up to. We felt the Japanese had to be planning something big. Of course I still believed we would be rescued any day, so I was not very worried.

The clothes I had been wearing for days were dirty and bloody and I stank so bad I was starting to smell myself. The lull gave me an opportunity to get some clean clothes. I drove to the barracks at Camp Two where I had left my things. The bed in the barracks looked very inviting, especially after sleeping on the ground for days. On one hand I wanted to lie down, and yet on the other I supported too much fear. Not even a feather bed could have enticed me to stay.

I grabbed clean clothes and drove directly to the lagoon. I did not want to put on clean clothes over a dirty body. I jumped into the lagoon to bathe and shave. I did not dillydally. I worried that the Japanese might surprise us and catch me naked as the day I was born. Even though I had to bathe without hot water, it felt marvelous to be clean again. I felt like a new man in clean clothes.

The only casualty we suffered that day was Captain Freuler's plane. On takeoff, the plane swerved and went wildly into dense underbrush. Freuler was all right, but the plane could not be repaired. In spite of losing a plane, all in all I considered it a good day.

Chapter Five

THE FOLLOWING DAY THE BOMBING RESUMED. Major Devereux kept telling us that help was on the way, except the help never materialized. Not only that, he kept changing the time. First help would be there in seventy-two hours, then he would tell us sixty, then forty-eight, and then back to seventy-two. I began to believe I was not being told the truth. It was becoming more and more difficult for me to keep the faith. Every man there felt if help did not arrive soon there was little hope we could keep surviving the enemy's ruthless attacks. Real anxiety crept into my very being when I began thinking that our country considered us expendable.

When bombs were not falling, construction could be heard about the island. Most civilians were busy building a new hospital underground, since the ammunition magazines was not large enough to hold all the wounded. Others tried to rebuild vital installations as fast as the Japanese destroyed them.

The civilians did whatever they were told to do and helped whenever and wherever they could. In spite of that, a few in the military did not think the civilians were doing enough. Being untrained in war, the civilians some time ended up in the way of the military operations. I thought the military's attitude of indifference and criticizing the civilian men was due to the desperate situation we were in. Even if every civilian had had a gun it would not have prevented the inevitable.

The only weapon the civilians had at hand was the power of prayer, and for many the only seemingly safe retreat was their foxholes. Even though many had not helped in the actual shooting, they tried to do their part and felt proud to be part of the team. The only real peace any of us knew was when sleep was granted us. I always fell asleep wishing that when I awakened reinforcements would be there to greet me. I refused to give up hope.

For a time the Japanese bombed at approximately the same time every-day. Then they began varying the bombings. By that time we were becoming veterans to their attacks. Daily bombings had become routine and waiting for help the national pastime. We had accepted that the Japanese were a persistent enemy and there was nothing more we could do to stop them.

Young men who were full of jokes and big talk a few days before were then melancholy and silent. Nobody was making fun or joking anymore about Japanese eyesight. Although for the amount of bombs the Japanese dropped, it was a wonder there was an island left to stand on. But eventually the law of averages was bound to take its toll. The Japanese got lucky and hit one of the big gun emplacements.

I took several civilians to Peacock Point to build underground shelters. The civilians still believed our government would never allow the Japanese to take Wake Island, despite the fact that Cunningham had already destroyed the United States codes and ordered all remaining coded material destroyed.

Johnny and I were kept busy hauling men to make repairs on the airstrip and driving supplies and ammunition to the gun emplacements. The nights were difficult enough trying to work in the dark, and the days were critical trying to get enough sleep between bombings. Through all that the military fought gallantly and survived unsurmountable odds.

Lieutenant Kinney and Lieutenant Kliewer took on a Japanese bomber formation the next day before they came into the range of our anti-aircraft guns. Even though Kinney and Kliewer had no luck, I believe they shook the Japanese up considerably because most of the bombs they dropped that day missed the island completely. Our anti-aircraft guns took a toll on them, too.

Just when we thought the bombing was over, a flying boat flew over and bombed Peale Island. I could not understand why the Japanese would use one of those planes. They were so slow and clumsy they made easy targets.

As if we did not have enough problems, the weather turned against us. A slow rain began. In light of our situation I was glad not to be in command. I heard rumors of stupid orders and messages coming from the supreme beings who had to be sitting on their brains to even issue such commands. I was told that Commander Cunningham was beside himself when he was told to continue dredging the channel so submarines could enter the lagoon and that Major Devereux was appalled when he received instructions to use seismographic paper for windows when the military did not have a building that was not lying in ruins. Did they think we were having a picnic or something? Every man on the island was needed for defense.

By the twentieth of December things were very desperate. That is when a navy PBY flew in from Honolulu with an important man on board doing an inspection tour of sorts. The men on that plane were so out of touch they wanted to know where the hotel was. Needless to say the marines were at a loss for words. One of the men pointed to a pile of debris and told them there it was. It was very apparent the men on the plane never had a clue how much damage Wake Island had sustained. I wanted to think they were kidding. It always bothered me to think the people who held my future in their hands were not as smart as me.

As a civilian my opinion did not mean spit. Still I would have liked to have had the opportunity to ask that inspector just where in the hell he had been the last two weeks and why had not any help been sent. The fact that I was stuck there expected to do my part, and yet I could not say anything galled me to the core.

The inspector brought a new ray of hope when he told us news of reinforcements. They were supposed to be on their way. That alone gave us hope that there still might be a rescue in the immediate future and our spirits soared.

The PBY was staying all night and men were told if they wanted to write letters, the PBY was taking all the mail and casualty lists out in the morning with Major Bayler, another important man on the island.

To keep track of the casualties, a large bulletin board had been put up. If someone knew about a death, they were to write the man's name on the bulletin board. It became routine for everyone to check that board periodically. I was told my name was on that board. I hurried to correct that mistake before my name was written on a casualty list. I did not want my family to think I had been killed.

One of the more humorous incidents occurred that morning. Remember the two Pan American employees that missed the plane on that first day? They had been through bombings and near-death experiences for two weeks. The PBY pilot told Mr. Hevenor he had room for one more. You never saw a happier man. Just before they were ready to take off, the pilot discovered they did not have a parachute or a life preserver for Mr. Hevenor, and it was against navy rules to fly without them, so the pilot told him that he could not go. It was not safe for him to fly without those safeguards. As if it was safer for him to stay on Wake Island! Mr. Hevenor was crestfallen for the second time. I know that was not funny for him, but when the rest of us heard that bit of news, we broke out laughing. Perish the thought that that pilot should break a rule.

When that PBY took off I watched it longingly until it flew out of sight. In less than two hours the skies were filled with Japanese bombers and they bombed us with a vengeance. Waves of fighters flew over and hit us with everything they had. Johnny and I knew then that we were not going get any help because those planes were from Japanese carriers.

Lieutenant Davidson bravely took off to meet the challenge. Captain Freuler was not far behind. They fought fearlessly and Freuler's plane was hit. He had to make a crash landing. Davidson never returned. Up until then the marines and the navy flyers had beaten off the enemy thrusts. But everyone knew by then we could not last much longer. Every hour then would be the last hour for many of us.

That night the military commandeered my truck. I was told I would not need it since we did not have to move the guns or haul supplies anymore. I knew with that statement there was no hope of being rescued. Johnny and I returned to the dugout to wait for the inevitable. I felt about as low as one can get. I was absolutely deflated. I could not help but wonder what tomorrow was going to be like.

The scuttlebutt was the marines were going to destroy the airfield and the big guns at the last minute to prevent the Japanese from using them. The one facility that either side never touched was the freshwater plant. If we had only known that. The fresh water plant proved to be the safest spot on the island.

At night we could see lights way out in the ocean. Of course I always prayed that was our navy, but it was not. It was the Japanese Navy's task force gearing up for battle.

I closed my eyes and silently prayed for a miracle. In spite of my big talk I was scared right down to my toes. I started to think of home again in an effort not to think about the present and what we might have to face tomorrow. My thoughts drifted to the time I first left home to be on my own.

DAD WANTED TO MOVE TO Arkansas, but Iva had just had another baby, so he had to wait. He always wanted to go to Arkansas ever since I could remember. My cousin John Rash was visiting us from Aspermont, Texas, about that time, and since I did not want to go to Arkansas, I saw my chance to be on my own. I told Dad I would much rather go to Texas with John and live with Aunt Rosie and Uncle Abe Rash. Aunt Rosie was Dad's sister. Since I would be living with relatives, I left home with Dad's blessings. I was in the eighth grade when I quit school. I bid a sad goodbye to my horse, Cherry. Skeet assured me he would take good care of Cherry, so I waved a touching yet happy farewell to all those I loved. I was barely fifteen.

When I arrived in Aspermont, Texas, I soon realized there were no jobs to be had and nobody had any money. Any dreams I fostered about finding work and becoming independently successful soon vanished.

While living in Aspermont, I learned of what I thought must be the worst job in the world, and that was driving the "honey wagon," or as some called it, "the tumble bug wagon." The honey wagon was equipped with a large tank that was made to hold the putrid fecal matter in outhouses. Uncle Abe lived in town, but they still had the traditional outhouse in back. Uncle Abe hired the man who drove a honey wagon to pump out the putrification hole in the outhouse once a month. The odor was most foul and so offensive I never understood how the man could tolerate the smell day after day after day.

I had been living in Texas for about six months when I received a letter etched in black. As soon as my eyes fell on that letter I knew it was not good news. My immediate thought was about Dad. My hands shook and my fingers trembled when I tore it open, almost too afraid to read the words inside. I read the baby had died, the baby who had been born just before I left home. Although I felt a certain sadness for Iva and Dad's loss, I experienced mixed emotions, for at the same time I felt so relieved that Dad was all right.

I packed what few belongings I owned and returned to New Mexico. I rode a freight train as far as possible and hitchhiked the rest of the way only to discover Dad and the family were no longer living there. They had finally moved to Arkansas. Let me add that hitchhiking and riding freight trains sure develops your sense of self preservation. You become very aware of those around you. My instincts became so perceptive when I felt I was in jeopardy, I would do a swift turnabout. I am sure I avoided many difficulties.

The cold, bitter winds of winter that chilled you to the bone descended upon the land and I was homeless. I tried for awhile to survive on my own. Each day the weather was getting worse and I was getting colder and hungrier. I was having a troublesome time just surviving. I had two uncles who lived a few miles away. Uncle Jim King and Aunt Bertha and Uncle Joe King and Aunt Nanny. I had to lay my pride aside and ask Uncle Joe for help.

I was lucky enough to get a ride with a truck driver who took me the twenty-five miles to Uncle Joe's. I looked forward to seeing my cousin Mac. He was a little older than me yet we always got along and had fun together.

Even though Uncle Joe and Aunt Nanny let me stay, it was a cold welcome. Uncle Joe was also having a very difficult time and I could sense that he was not very happy about me living there. Although he did not say anything to me about it, Uncle Joe's actions spoke louder than any words. There were many times the silence was deafening and I felt very much unwanted. I became very aware that I was accepted only because I was family and it was in the middle of winter. However, Mac was happy, even excited, about my living with him. In no time at all we became as close as brothers.

Two months later Uncle Joe secured a job on a large ranch quite a few miles from there. He stored their household furniture in an old warehouse in Hagerman and moved away. That left me without a place to live. Mac wanted to stay with me and be on his own. Uncle Joe did not like that idea but finally gave into Mac's wishes.

Mac was a great cousin. He had the persona of a gentleman. He controlled his emotions and it took a lot to make him mad. He was soft spoken and very polite. Mac and I developed a strong bond between us and we had a powerful sense of duty to one another.

Mac and I wandered around for days without any shelter from the cold. We decided we had to find a place to live. We returned to the warehouse where Uncle Joe had his furniture stacked to the rafters. We dug out a bed and made a little spot to set it up. At last we had a place to sleep. We still did not have any heat, but at least we were inside and out of the weather.

Steady jobs were scarce. If I made ten cents a day working in the pool hall racking balls, I felt lucky. Everyday was a challenge just to survive. Hunger was our constant companion. Mac and I lived one day at a time and we never worried about the future, only what tomorrow might bring. The only thing I had going for me was I possessed the tenacity of a weed.

That warehouse was home throughout the winter. By springtime Mac and I had been confined inside for so long we felt restless. Even though we did not have the money we decided to visit Mac's parents, who lived a hundred twenty-five miles west of Roswell, New Mexico. Mac wanted to borrow his brother's 1931 Model A Roadster to make the trip, but he lived miles away in Hobbs, New Mexico, the oil center of the state.

I talked Mac into hitchhiking to Hobbs. Mac never liked to hitchhike and complained about it all the way. When I pointed out how much money we were saving by not taking a bus, Mac felt a little better about the power of the thumb.

Mac's brother Jim knew we did not have very much money, and he filled the gas tank before turning over the keys to us. Mac and I thanked him over and over for his thoughtfulness. We waved a happy goodbye and left Hobbs with our spirits high and a song in our hearts. Mac and I thought that was our lucky day.

That Model A Roadster was a real pretty little thing. We knew that Jim took goad care of it and so must we. As we were driving through Roswell, Mac stopped at a stop sign. The car locked up. Mac backed up about a hundred feet and the car locked up again. Mac raced the motor and let out the clutch. When he did that the gears came loose and busted the transmission housing. Pieces of metal flew in every direction.

We did not have any money to have the car fixed, and we realized it was our responsibility to have it repaired. After all, we had borrowed it. We pushed the car to the side of the road and left it until we could figure out what we should do. Mac finally screwed up enough courage to let Jim know that his pride and joy was sitting along the road needing a good mechanic. Jim was upset when he received the news, yet he never blamed us. And for that we were thankful.

Jim made arrangements to have the Model A pulled to a garage. He told us it would not be fair for Mac and I to pay a hundred percent for the repairs. He had had the car for a long time and he offered to pay a third. I felt that I was sure blessed with wonderful cousins. It was as if a heavy burden had been lifted off our shoulders after we told Jim. Of course Mac and I still had the worry of paying our share of the repairs.

The rancher whom Uncle Joe worked for lived in Roswell. His name was Judd McKnight and he turned out to be a nice fellow. Mac and I walked to his house and introduced ourselves. We explained that we were stranded. He told us that he was going to the ranch the following morning and he would be happy to take us with him if we wanted to go. He even invited us to stay the night, and Mac and I happily agreed.

The next morning while traveling to the ranch we told Mr. McKnight what a jam we were in and he offered us a job that paid fifty cents a day with room and board. Mac and I quickly accepted before he could change his mind. I thought we had it made since we would be working with Uncle Joe and I was eager to start.

Uncle Joe was happy to see us. When Judd told Joe that he had given us a job, Joe's expression changed. As soon as Uncle Joe had Mac and me alone, he warned us not to expect any special treatment because we were family. In fact to make him proud, we had to work twice as hard as anybody else. So much for thinking I had it made.

I WAS BROUGHT TO REALITY when a bomb exploded nearby. The bombing was heavy. The island was surrounded by a Japanese armada. Scuttlebutt was the Japanese had landed on the other side of the island. I could hear rapid gunfire coming from every direction. The marines fought with everything they had and the Japanese suffered heavy losses. I was so scared I felt sick all over. I lay in that dugout wishing I could pull it over me. I knew the end was near and I prayed for the courage to face death with honor and withstand whatever lay ahead.

There was rapid gunfire throughout that night and the Japanese shelling was heavy. Many shells hit the island and almost as many blew up in the lagoon or missed the island completely, landing in the ocean. I prayed again for another miracle since I considered every hour the marines were able to hold against such a determined enemy was a miracle.

The dawn revealed the Japanese onslaught was too great and the marines were forced to surrender. Any dreams of being wealthy in the future or even having a future was squashed. The thought occurred to me that Wake Island was sure properly named.

A man came to the dugout to inform us the island was in Japanese hands and we were to walk to the road with our hands clasp over our heads. An avalanche of mixed emotions fell over me like a blanket. The pangs of intense overwhelming fear were paralyzing. My legs shook so I could hardly stand. I broke out in a cold sweat because I thought death was in my immediate future. I clasped my hands over my head and I forced one foot in front of the other as I silently prayed for courage.

I was terrified of what lay ahead and yet there was a certain amount of relief knowing the fighting was over. I prayed that if it was meant for me to die that it should be quick rather than be subjected to lingering torture.

I still could not believe that America had not come to our defense. It was as if nobody cared what happened to us. In spite of those terrible thoughts I still clung to the belief that the Japanese were going to be very sorry someday for what they were doing.

The weather was appropriately overcast for the occasion. The smell of rain was in the air. I felt absolutely forsaken as I slowly walked downtrodden as a man would on his way to the gallows. Then I thought I was hearing things when I heard, "Psst, psst," coming from the brush about ten feet from me. When I investigated it was another civilian. He wanted me to stay in the brush and resist capture with him and a few other civilians. Although their cause was just, it was futile to resist at that point. Later my fears proved right because those who resisted were shot.

When the eight of us walked out of the brush and onto the road we joined an unknown number of men. Everyone had their hands locked over their heads. At least I was not alone in my misery. Being with them gave me the courage to face my enemy with a certain amount of pride, even though I was shaking from head to toe. The old saying "Misery loves company" was never so unmistakably true. Some men staggered with eyes glazed in disbelief. Some walked with pride and stares of hate. Some fell and those that could not get up were bayoneted where they fell.

There were five or six pickup trucks with machine guns mounted on the top and a Japanese soldier standing behind every gun in a ready to fire stance. The machine guns looked like our .30-caliber machine guns. Two more Japanese soldiers were standing in the bed of the pickup with guns. Their hatred for us was so potent I could sense it in the air. I looked into the face of my enemy and they all wore expressions of pure loathing. I had the feeling they wanted to shoot us right there.

I looked around to see if the Japanese were using my green truck and I did not see it anywhere. After practically living in that hunk of machinery for two weeks, I could not help but wonder what had happened to it.

With our hands clasped over our heads, we were marched to that large hole in the ground that was to be the new hospital the civilians had been building. It was about forty feet wide and one hundred fifty feet long.

The Japanese used the Hawaiians who could understand Japanese as interpreters. Two Hawaiians were standing by the front of that large hole and told us to remove all our clothes and personal effects such as rings and watches.

The entrance that led down into that hole was sloped, and from the outside I could not see anything. But I knew that hole was about fifteen or twenty feet deep since I had brought work crews there almost everyday. There was a huge pile of clothes at the side of the entrance so I knew many others must already be down there.

Once the Japanese soldiers were satisfied that we were not trying to hide anything, we were shoved toward the entrance. I was stark naked when I walked down the slope into that hole. There must have been at least one hundred fifty men sitting down, all naked as the day they were born. Seeing so many of my friends still alive was a welcomed sight. We had to sit in close ranks and get as close as possible to keep making more room as more prisoners were brought in. We ended up with about four hundred men in that hole.

When I looked up I saw four heavier machine guns that were set up around the top edge of the hole pointing down toward us. Those guns looked like our .50-caliber machine guns. I had hoped to make it home someday, but I changed my mind right there and then. I knew we were put in that hole naked so they could shoot us and shove the dirt over us. The fear of dying returned and I shook all over. Thoughts of everything I had left undone passed through my mind. If only I could see my dad and family just one more time.

Chapter Six

WHISPERED PRAYERS COULD BE HEARD AROUND ME. I was sure that hole was going to be my grave and any needs or wants ceased to occupy my thoughts. Instead my concerns drifted to my own mortality. Never before had it been so clear to me how precious life really was than it was at that moment. I had come to the end of my life and I prayed silently for another miracle. I did not want to die and my emotions were at the lowest ebb they had ever been. I had known fear many times, but it was not until then that I experienced sheer terror from the depths of my being.

I chastised myself again for coming to Wake Island in the first place. Why had not I listened to Donna and stayed home? I told myself, "Here I am on this God-forsaken little coral island that I never even heard of before I came. I will undoubtedly be killed here. I will never see my folks again and they will never know where I am buried." There was nothing in the world to keep me from thinking anything else.

I knew I had to stop thinking about death—it was too disheartening. I started thinking more positive thoughts. I told myself every minute was precious and I figured as long as I was alive there was hope. Never before had I thought about time, especially minute by minute. And I regretted all the time I had wasted in my life doing foolish things—time that I could never make up or relive. My mind was spinning in nonsensical things trying not to think about the present.

We were not to talk to each other, and to keep myself from breaking down completely and maintain a certain amount of dignity, I tried not to think about where I was. I wondered what Mac was doing. I remembered how terrible Mac and I thought we had it when we were grubbing loco weed. How I wished I could have those days again. I was so deep into recollection I could almost smell the mesquite.

WHEN MAC AND I WERE working on the ranch with Uncle Joe, our job was grubbing loco weed, and we thought that was beneath us. We could not complain about it because of Uncle Joe. Evidently my attitude was showing because the older ranch hands kidded me about it. Yet on the other hand they always looked after Mac and me. It was just their way of helping me grow up.

One day I bravely told Mr. McKnight that Mac and I were not satisfied, so Judd gave us the job of breaking wild mustangs. When Uncle Joe was told that Mac and I were the new bronc-busters, he just shook his head in wonderment and belly laughed. That alone made me more determined than ever to be the best bronc-buster ever. No matter how many horses we broke, we still only made fifty cents a day. So there was no incentive to break any more horses than we had to.

Mac had never been exposed to breaking horses and he had quite a bad time handling the raw power of wild mustangs. I was raised on ranches so breaking horses was not new to me.

After awhile I became rather cocky. I felt there was not a horse I could not handle. Like a bantam rooster, I strutted around the ranch. No one had yet told me the old adage, "Pride goes before a fall."

One day Judd told Mac and me to ride out and pick up some tools that had been left out on the range. There was one mustang in the corral that needed more training. I snubbed him down and saddled him. Mac rode a big brown quarter horse.

When we found the tools I got off my horse to pick them up. I handed the tools to Mac and tried to remount my horse. That mustang would not let me back on no matter what I did. Every time I started to remount, that horse would whirl to kick me. After several attempts to remount, I was ready to shoot that mustang, except I did not have a gun.

The mustang was snorting, breathing hard, and scared. Suddenly he whirled away from me and jumped against Mac's big brown horse. The big horse slipped in a prairie dog hole with a hind foot and fell down with Mac on him. The mustang jumped over Mac and the big horse only to land on Mac's leg with two of his hind feet. The blood spurted from Mac's leg. Both horses were wild-eyed and took off leaving Mac lying on the ground.

I ran to Mac and helped him up. He was very lucky that no bones were broken. The blood was running down Mac's leg and over the side of his foot. I bound his leg with my bandana handkerchief. We were miles away from the ranch and I cussed like an old sailor because of the predicament in which we found ourselves. For a cowboy, losing your horse was just about the worse thing that could happen.

Mac could not stand without leaning on me. It was all I could do to hold him up. For awhile I worried that Mac might bleed to death before we reached the ranch. Thanks to my bandana that did not happen. With Mac leaning on me, he slowly hobbled back to the ranch.

That incident sure humbled my inflated ego. I was really embarrassed about losing my horse and having to walk back to the ranch. When Mac and I entered the bunkhouse the other cowhands sure gave us a hootering over that episode. Mac and I never tried again to retrieve those tools. Those tools could still be there for all I know.

When Mac and I had finally made enough money to pay our share of the repairs on Jim's car, we quit Judd McKnight. We got a lift to the garage in Roswell and picked up the Model A. After paying our share, we still had enough money to rent an unfurnished room in Roswell from an old lady who lived alone.

The only piece of furniture in the room was an old wood stove. So before returning the car to Jim, Mac and I drove to Hagerman and raided the warehouse where Uncle Joe and Aunt Nanny still had their things stored. We rustled a bed, table, and chairs to furnish our room. We returned the car and gave Jim a hearty thank you. Despite Mac's aversion to hitchhiking, to save money we thumbed our way home. Our families were so well known in the area I never had to wait very long for a ride.

We were confident of finding work since President Franklin Delano Roosevelt had created an organization called the WPA, which guaranteed everyone a job. That was a lifesaver for the poor and, as a matter of fact, the whole country. Franklin D. Roosevelt was considered a saint by the working man.

We secured a job on an FFA project building houses. The FFA was another government program. I was anything but a carpenter, so I was put to shingling roofs. I was not very good at that, either. I still managed to keep that job until the FFA project came to an end.

When winter arrived Mac and I were without a job. We still had rent to pay so we had to watch every penny we had. We did not have any wood for the stove and tried burning newspapers to heat the room. We spent hours rolling the newspapers up tightly, but they just smoked and smouldered around the edges and did not generate any lasting heat. When we loosened the papers they burned so quickly they never produced any lasting heat, either.

Mac and I knew we had to find some wood, and we needed Jim's car again to do that. That same 1931 Model A Roadster. Jim told us to try and keep it in one piece. I thought it was very charitable of Jim to let us borrow his car again, especially after what happened the last time he let us use it.

We already knew that finding any trees or wood to burn was not going to be easy. We felt sure if we drove north of Roswell we would find some scrubby trees. However, Mac and I drove for miles and we became very discouraged when we had not found any wood of any kind.

It was at that time an idea hit me. There was a fence running along the side of the road we were driving on. In desperation I told Mac my wild idea.

We could remove every other fence post and nobody would ever know the difference. Mac thought my idea held merit so that is what we did.

Mac opened the rumble seat and we loaded as many posts as possible. We stood them upright and then used those posts to hold more posts stacked crosswise. We stacked them as high as we dared without them falling off and tied them down. On one hand I said a silent prayer that we would not get caught. Yet on the other I gave thanks that at last we had some wood to burn. We would not have to sit around any more with our coats on and shiver to keep warm.

We made two trips and I thought we had enough posts to last us through the coldest part of the winter. We did not dare return Jim's car as dirty as it was. We washed, swept, brushed the seats, and had everything shinning like new when we returned the car to Jim the following day. Of course neither of us mentioned that we had used the car to haul dirty fence posts. We filled the gas tank and told Jim thanks and then hitchhiked seventy-five miles back to Roswell.

We had been so cold for so long that Mac and I kept that wood stove burning brightly night and day. It was not long until we were out of wood and had to borrow Jim's car again and repeat the whole process. We never mentioned to Jim what we were using his car for.

Mac and I returned to the same fence. Again, I said another silent prayer for a safe getaway. That time we hauled even more fence posts home. We removed every other fence post until we reached the end of the fence and then we started all over again. My conscience was bothering me but not enough to stop me from removing every other fence post. When we drove away, the fence posts that were left were so far apart the fence wire was lying on the ground.

Mac and I knew that was not the right thing to do, however, it was freezing cold so we did it anyway. We just counted our blessings that we were never caught and we used the wood sparingly after that. We had spent the last bit of our money on groceries and we were flat broke. If winter did not come to an end soon, Mac and I did not know what we were going to do.

Finally the weather changed and Mac and I were able to find an odd job here and there. Imagine how we felt when we hired out for a two-day work detail with several other men to build a fence. The same fence we had taken the posts from. I felt just a twinge of guilt, and yet I was so desperate for money I counted my blessings. I told Mac it would seem the Lord does help those who help themselves. While Mac and I worked we made light of the whole situation. Yet underneath all the jokes and smiles, I fostered mixed emotions over that fence and I tried to justify the theft.

I do not know who I was trying to convince since it was probably the mysterious ways of the mutable Fates that brought that about. For whatever the reason, it was great to have a little money to live on again.

The sun finally had some warmth to it, and the vernal season spread across the land announcing that spring was coming. The warmer days brought about the loveliness of spring blossoms. All the birds and animals were filled with the mating instinct and Mac and I were no different. Mac met a young lady named Faye Mitchell who captured his heart, and he decided he was ready to give up his bachelor existence. It was not very long until he and Faye were married, leaving me once again alone and on my own. Mac and Faye were happily married and remained together all their lives.

For someone who tried so hard to be on his own, I hated being alone. And yet in spite of all the negatives of being alone, I relished my independence.

I knew I had to move; I could not pay the rent on the room Mac and I had. When Mac moved out he returned the bed, table, and chairs to his folks. I packed my few things and walked into town to find a job. I did not care what I had to do as long as it was honest work.

I hated that deep feeling of melancholy that hung over my head like a heavy pall when I did not have any money coming in. And just the thought of money brought me to immediate reality. The want of money is what brought me to Wake Island.

"MONEY," I REPEATED TO MYSELF. By the time I realized that money was not the most a important thing in life, it was too late. Money was no longer of great importance to me. The reality of what was really important became very apparent: God, family, and loved ones. Money could not help me escape. I chastised myself again for ever coming to that God-forsaken tiny island of Wake. I promised myself that if I should survive, I would never again let the quest for money take me away from my family.

Seeing the desperation on the many faces around me made me realize I was not alone, and somehow that gave me the strength I needed to control myself. Once I had accepted that the Grim Reaper was standing in my shadow and death was just a doorway to another part of life, a certain peace beyond human understanding came over me. There was not anything else the Japanese could do to scare me anymore than I had already been.

We sat there about three or four hours in quiet desperation. The Japanese came in and took about fifty men out. We could not see anything on the outside from down in that hole, and every once in awhile we could hear machine-gun fire and rifles being shot here and there in the distance. We really thought the Japanese had taken those fifty men and executed them. I could not understand why they would do that when they already had us penned up like rats in that hole. Why would they march men out and shoot them in the open? I came to the conclusion there was something else going on. I just could not figure out what.

Time passed slowly and nothing happened. We were left to sit there as if forgotten. We had to relieve ourselves as best we could where we were. It was very embarrassing and sickening to be treated like an animal.

I have often wondered to this day why somebody did not lunge one of those Japanese guards and kill as many as we could before they killed us. But we did not, and that was the luckiest thing that ever happened.

Later that afternoon we were herded outside and told to dress. That was pretty embarrassing too. Several men were so scared they had soiled their pants and we were not given any time to pick out clothes. We were forced to grab whatever we could, whether it fit or not. By the time I could get near the pile, the only piece of clothing left was a pair of shorts and an old pair of shoes that were too big. That pair of shorts was the only piece of clothing between me and nakedness. Of course all the rings, watches, and other jewelry were gone forever.

The weather had turned chilly and it had started raining. We were marched to the airport under heavy guard over the same road I had driven so many times. The Japanese were not taking any chances of our escaping. Guards were placed about every ten feet around us. We were not allowed to talk or even help another prisoner in need. We were treated with bitter contempt, as if they were mad because we were still alive and they were having to deal with us.

We had walked about a mile when we came upon one of the ammunition magazines that was being used for a temporary hospital. The Japanese guards stopped us. The steps leading down to the door of the magazine was blocked preventing entry. Evidently that magazine had been overlooked until then.

A Hawaiian told the Japanese guard it was being used as a hospital. A few of the prisoners were made to clear the steps. The entry was built in an L-shape, and although we could not see the door, we could sure hear the bullets hit it. The guards machine-gunned that heavy metal door several times. Then the guard yelled, "Come out. Come out."

The door opened slowly and the doctors came out. Surprisingly, nobody inside that magazine was hit by the Japanese volley of bullets. The doctors' skin was pasty looking from being underground so long and they had beards. It was obvious they needed rest. Those who were wounded and could walk were helping the ones that could not make it on their own. After everyone had stripped and had been checked for weapons, they were allowed to dress. Guards were left to watch the more seriously wounded who could not travel and had to be left behind with a doctor.

I had another friend beside Johnny McCloud, also named Johnny, who was from Grants Pass. I knew he had been wounded, but I did not know how bad or what had become of him. I saw that he was amongst the wounded who were being helped. I tried to make my way to him without being noticed. Before I could reach him, Johnny sat and fell over. He was so weak with dysentery he could not get up. Before anyone could move to help him, a Japanese soldier put his foot on the side of his head and stuck a bayonet in his neck then cut Johnny's throat. I turned cold with horror. Seeing that sure did not help my emotions.

We started marching again, and I had a hard time keeping up with those uncomfortable big shoes I was wearing, though I dared not say a word. I sure did not want to draw attention to myself especially when I thought about Johnny. My mind kept returning to the horror of seeing his throat cut without hesitation.

I walked along with my head down, watching the ground as though I was in a trance. Like a robot, I put one foot in front of the other. I was not paying much attention to anything. I guess I was still in shock over what had happened to Johnny. Another fella who was walking two men ahead of me was bayonetted and killed right there with abandoned fury and vigor. I had no idea what he had done to deserve that. Nonetheless, that incident sure brought me to attention.

To be killed for nothing was nerve-racking and disheartening. I had to exert every emotional resource I could gather to calm my fears. I wondered if I was going to be able to withstand their inhuman treatment.

We arrived at the airport about five in the evening. There must have been a thousand men sitting there on the tie-down. Behind the men was a bank about ten or twelve feet high made of sand where it had been scooped up to make a wind break for the planes when they were tied down. There were big machine-guns mounted upon that bank for a hundred yards and pointing down at us. There were other machine-guns mounted on trucks that were placed around the perimeter pointing at us from all sides. I could not help but wonder what the Japanese had in mind for us. My dreams of living a long life were much in doubt.

Instead of shooting us, the Japanese just left us sitting in the rain. All of us were soaked to the skin. Of course in my case, that was all I had covering me besides a pair of shorts. It was a wonder I never came down with pneumonia or simply dropped dead from fear—and that is how I faced those first hours of Japanese occupation.

Commander Cunningham, Major Devereux, and Dan Teters were questioned extensivly. The Japanese could not believe that we did not have radar and so few guns. They were thoroughly convinced that we must have had more guns. They also held resentment toward Cunningham for saying, "Send us more Japs."

Commander Cunningham was given credit earlier in the war for saying that and he always proclaimed that his superiors had misunderstood the message. The Japanese finally took Cunningham at his word. In fact, the Japanese interrogator who questioned Cunningham was educated at one of the finest universities in America. He confidentially told Cunningham it was great propaganda.

Just before dark the Japanese took the American cooks to the kitchen at Camp Two. They were to prepare something to eat for us. One corner of the

51

kitchen had been bombed and there was loose pieces of tin hanging and lying all over. While the cooks were baking bread the wind came up and started rattling the tin and causing a number of odd noises. The Japanese became real scared and pushed the cooks back into the trucks with their bayonets and returned them to the airport. The Japanese were still afraid of us and thought the cooks might try something during the storm, so we never received anything to eat or drink that first night.

That night George Kelly found me in the crowd and gave me a pair of new khaki pants and shirt. I do not know how he came to have them, but I was so thankful to get them I never asked questions. Those clothes saved me from the misery of being chilled to the bone. I was finally able to trade those big shoes to someone who had shoes that were too small.

I saw Melvin Davidson, who was a good friend of mine, and he told me the night the Japanese landed he had been loading the belts for the machine guns on Wilkes Island. When Mel finished, he walked along the beach to return to Wake and his foxhole. Mel never saw or heard anything out of the ordinary. The ferry was closed and he had to cross the channel hand-over-hand on the cable. Mel counted his blessings when he was told later that not very long after he had walked that beach, the Japanese ran two large ships aground in order to land their troops safely.

Johnny McCloud and I had gotten separated in the mass exodus to the airport, so it would be a long time before I would see him again—and then it was from a distance. At least I knew he was still alive.

Darkness enveloped us and the night was chilly. I tried to rest the best I could on that hard tarmac. I was wet, cold, and hungry. I spent the most miserable long hours of my young life that night. Throughout the night moans of desperation could be heard and I never knew if someone was hurt or being killed. I prayed several times during the night for a miracle and I was not alone. I am quite sure there were many who prayed in silence that night.

Too bad we could not have heard the tribute then that was later paid to the men who fought on Wake Island by Masatake Okumiya, Commander of the Japanese Imperial Navy. He said considering the power accumulated for the invasion of Wake Island and meager forces of the defenders, it was one of the most humiliating defeats the Japanese had ever suffered. At the time of surrender we were so deflated by *our* defeat that we never considered how costly their victory really was for them.

Chapter Seven

IT TOOK ALL THE INNER STRENGTH I COULD GATHER TO keep from crying.
I lay down and tried desperately to find a comfortable position on that hard
tarmac. Under the circumstances I found that sleeping was impossible. I
was wide awake to watch the first streaks of dawn appear on the horizon
only to disappear under a blanket of heavy, dark rain clouds, and the rain
fell in torrents.

Because of the heavy rains we were moved into the plane revetments.
However, we were so many in such a close area, it was not very long before
we used up all the oxygen and men began fainting. Because of the courage
of one man who knew a few Japanese words and pleaded to have us moved,
we were herded back out into the rain onto the airport's tarmac.

The cooks were once again allowed to return to the kitchen to fix food
for us while the rest of us sat out in the weather on that cold, hard tarmac
all day. I welcomed the warm sun that appeared intermittently through the
clouds. After awhile the sun became too hot and I welcomed the clouds. We
would no more dry out and another rain squall would hit us. Unsettled
weather continued for most of the day.

The time passed ever so slowly. Periodically the Japanese took work
crews to do whatever. The scuttlebutt was they were building barbed-wire
fences around the barracks at Camp Two.

It was hard to believe it was the Christmas holidays. There was nothing
to remind us of those Holy days. In fact to even mention them would have
probably generated your immediate death. Finally the rain let up and I was
so exhausted from not doing anything but sit, I was finally able to get a short
nap lying on that tarmac.

That evening the Japanese brought us the bread the cooks had baked.
They also brought jelly and cheese. Each of us were given a small piece of

bread about half as big as a biscuit with two bites of cheese or a spoonful of jelly. They also gave us a cup of water out of those barrels that we had filled up, and it tasted like gasoline. I was so thirsty I did not care how it tasted. I gulped it down.

I had not eaten since before we surrendered so that biscuit and jelly tasted gourmet to me. I savored that biscuit and jelly and made it last as long as possible. There were many who complained about that, but to my way of thinking, as long as the Japanese gave us food, they wanted to keep us alive. And for that I was thankful.

My thoughts wandered to home and family. I thought of the traditional turkey dinner I would be eating if I were home. I recalled how miserable I would feel after every holiday meal from overeating. I prayed I would survive to enjoy those good times again.

Another long miserable night had to be endured while the Japanese figured out what to do with us. We stayed in close ranks to keep warm. The night was anything but pleasant if you could not sleep. Sleep brought forgetfulness; that was the only way to escape reality and the present situation. So no matter how uncomfortable I was on that tarmac, I finally succumbed to sleep.

In the morning I was stiff and sore from lying on that unaccustomed hard surface. The sun finally made a welcomed appearance. Despite all the misery and destruction that could be seen in every direction, the sunshine made everything seem a little better than it really was.

We were given another hard biscuit with a little jelly and a very small piece of cheese for breakfast. We were also given another cup of that gasoline-tasting water with which to wash it down. Instead of the annihilation that I felt would surely take place, we were being kept alive. For whatever the reason it was apparent they wanted to use us for something, and my hopes were renewed that I was going to live.

Soon after that so-called breakfast the Japanese colonel in charge of the island made a speech. He told us that he had received word not to kill us. And as long as we obeyed and did not cause any trouble, we would live. Sighs of relief could be heard across the tarmac. To my way of thinking the Japanese meant to kill us when we were in that hole. Maybe I had my miracle after all and I never realized it at the time.

Work crews were taken to look for the dead. There were still hundreds of dead Japanese soldiers that had to be undressed and piled in a heap to burn. And it was important to dispose of those bodies as soon as possible for obvious reasons. What a way to spend Christmas.

Another work party was formed to search for the parts to the big guns the marines had thrown away. It was hard to believe that the Japanese would really think we would turn over those parts should we find them. However, the men put on a good show of searching.

Toward nightfall another miracle of sorts occurred. We were marched under heavy guard to the barracks at Camp Two. The barracks had been encircled by barbed wire. I could not believe it when I was allowed to stay in my own barracks and we were given hot spaghetti for dinner. I was permitted to have soap, a tooth brush, and tooth paste. I was shocked when they even let me keep my razor. Things were looking up.

With our cooks in the kitchen, from then on we were given two meals a day. Oatmeal in the morning and soup or sandwiches or spaghetti for dinner. We were being fed the captured rations of our own lauder.

Most everyday the Japanese guards came in and rounded up as many men as needed for work crews and marched them out. I tried to stay out of sight. For the first time in my life I was glad to be considered a man of samll stature. I never stood out in a lineup so I was passed over time after time.

The work crews were to rebuild what the bombs had destroyed. One work crew was formed strictly for cleanup. One of the prisoners found a bottle of whiskey and drank it all. He became so intoxicated he could not work. The Japanese tied his hands behind him and cut his head off with a saber right there on the spot, so we knew they meant business and we could not kid around. When we were told not to do something, we did not do it.

Those who knew construction formed a work crew inside the barracks. They repaired the water lines and restored the showers and toilet facilities. Life was returning to some kind of order, although we still did not have any electricity.

A few days later we were given a four-or-five-page questionnaire to fill out. They were mostly interested in those who were mechanics, welders, or carpenters. Since I was not any good at any of those jobs, I did not qualify for anything.

We were questioned, too. The Japanese wanted to know what our jobs were on Wake Island and what other qualifications we had. I told them I was the garbage man and sometime I helped in the kitchen. In today's world I would have had an important-sounding title such as sanitation engineer or something like that—but I would still be a garbage man. I also told them that I was very good at branding and roping cattle and breaking horses. The Japanese were not impressed with me at all.

It was their practice to ask all kinds of questions and expect immediate answers. In the beginning any prisoner who caused trouble was either stabbed or shot. Later the shootings stopped and the beatings began. To wear a black eye became a status symbol.

There was one prisoner named Noka-nish-ni, who was Japanese-American. I am not sure of the spelling, but phonetically that is what it sounded like. The Japanese commander tried his best to convert Nokanishni to the Imperials way of thinking but he failed. Nokanishni refused to cooperate and, since he was Japanese, he suffered a double whammy and was beaten unmercifully. He had taken more punishment than any of us. Nokanishni had the respect and sympathy of all of us. He was truly an all-American boy and had the cuts and bruises to prove it.

My heart burned with resentment towards the Japanese. How could they be so cruel even to their own? That such things could take place in a so-called civilized world and go unpunished was the bitter reality of being a prisoner of war.

As those first uncertain days of our imprisonment passed, the mistreatment and beatings let up a little. I began to notice things about the Japanese military. The commanding officers were just as hard on their own men as they were on the prisoners. Not that that made it any easier for us, but it gave me a better understanding of my enemy.

After the first week the Japanese commander relaxed many restrictions and we were allowed to play cards, read, or walk around and talk openly with the other men. Of course we were still confined behind barbed wire, but routines had been established. We knew the boundaries of what we could and could not do. Even an attitude of cordialness had developed between some prisoners and the guards.

In spite of the better treatment, every time I thought about Johnny and how he was killed, of Nokanishni and the senseless killings I had witnessed the resentment that I held toward the Japanese was rekindled. My feelings of dislike for the Japanese were burned deep into the very soul of my being, and I still believed they were going to be very sorry for their actions some-day. I prayed to a higher justice, to avenge us.

The weather turned chilly. I tried to think of more pleasant days, the days of my adventurous youth. The weather was also chilly the day Mac arid I parted to go our separate ways.

A COLD NORTH WIND WAS blowing the day I walked into town to look for work. I noticed several homeless men on the street and thought if any jobs were available, they would not be standing around. I held little hope of finding any work.

I passed the men hurriedly, as if I had a place to go. I rounded the corner and ran headlong into my little niece, Evelyn, who was Velma's daughter. I asked her where her mother was. Evelyn told me that Velma was in the grocery store.

After being on my own for months, my clothes looked threadbare. Although my clothes and body were clean, I had that down-in-the-heels look. I never realized what a sad picture I projected until I saw the look on Velma's face when she came out of the grocery store. She took one look at me and gasped, "Lloyd. Where did you come from?"

"Gosh it is good to see you, Sis. I was looking for a job."

"If you are not doing anything, come home with me. I could use some help."

"It has been a long time since I enjoyed a home-cooked meal."

"Come on then. Dallas should be here to pick me up at any minute."
Without giving the matter any thought, I accepted most happily.

"I have a surprise for you at home," Velma said.

I could not imagine what she was talking about so I asked, "What?"

"Dad left Cherry with me when the family moved to Arkansas."

"That is the best news I have had for a long time." My spirits were lifted because the thought had crossed my mind that Dad might have sold Cherry when he moved.

Dallas pulled up in an old rattle-trap of a car and when he saw me he cried out, "Well if you are not a sight for sore eyes."

"I am glad to see you too," I replied laughing.

When Velma told Dallas I was coming home with them, Dallas was happy about that. He told me that since he was always away from home trading horses or whatever he could find to make a little money and since it was quite a ways between neighbors, he was glad I would be there with Velma and Evelyn for awhile.

Dallas and Velma had homesteaded a section. Six hundred forty acres of rabbit-eaten land that was not good for anything. Even if you tried you could not raise a good case of hell on it. They were the last of the homesteaders in New Mexico.

I stayed with Velma, even though I found there was not very much for me to do. Velma worried about me, and to keep me from leaving she kept creating things for me to fix. I could see what she was up to. I did not know what to do about it. I loved my sister, but I needed a paying job. In spite of her good intentions, I knew I would have to leave soon.

The son of another homesteader, named Ross Ledbetter, who was a friend of mine in grade school, came by on a big gray horse to ask if I wanted to ride with him to look for work. I was more than happy to go with him. I quickly saddled up Cherry. It felt good to be back in the saddle again.

Russ and I rode from ranch to ranch without any luck. On the third day we were about to call it quits when we rode upon the ranch of June Tulk. He had known Dad and the family for years. June and his wife Jerrie were two of the nicest people anyone could ever want to meet. June was working alone in the corral. As soon as he saw Ross and me, he knew what we wanted and said, "You boys look tired. Get down and rest awhile."

"Thanks. I sure could use a drink of water," I replied.

"Put your horses in the corral over there and feed them. Go up to the cook-shack and get something to eat with the other men," June instructed.

"Thanks again," I replied.

"Soon as you finish come to ranch house and talk to me," June ordered.

Ross and I unsaddled our horses and put them in the corral. After we gave fresh hay to our horses, we hurried to the cook-house. Not only to eat, but we wanted to get acquainted with the other men since we were sure we had a job. It was that time of year when lambing was starting.

When we finished eating we moseyed back to the corral and saddled our horses. Ross and I were feeling real confident we had found work. We rode to the ranch house to receive our orders. When June told us he did not need any help right then, I was so disappointed it must have shown in my face because before I could say anything he asked if we could come back in two weeks.

"You can count on me Mr. Tulk," I said, and Ross shook his head in agreement saying, "Me too."

"Call me June. I will expect you then in two weeks. I can use your horses, too."

After Ross and I rode away from June Tulk's place, the men told June that they thought I was too small to handle the job. June bet them a month's wages I would be the best hand between Ross and me. Later when I was told about that, I felt pretty good and about three feet taller.

I was never very big and always underweight. I guess you might say I was the Tom Thumb of the family. Because of my size I looked to be about thirteen years old. But I was wiry and not afraid of hard work.

The next two weeks passed ever so slowly for me. Probably because I was so anxious to leave my sister's and get a life of my own back. I could hardly wait to go to work and have a paycheck coming in again. Two days before that two weeks was up, Ross came by and we decided we should leave a day early. Ross and I were not taking any chances of being late and losing the jobs to somebody else.

June Tulk kept one man named J.R. Lockheart all year around. During lambing, June hired sixteen men. When lambing was over, he laid off everyone except his one steady hand, so Ross and I knew the job was only temporary.

When we arrived at the ranch, June put Ross in the day corral and asked me if I knew how to cut sheep.

"I know how to cut calves. I guess you cut them the same way," I replied.

"I am not talking about marking them. I want to separate them," June said.

"I can do that," I replied.

June began explaining about his sheep herds. He tried to keep approximately sixty to seventy sheep in one herd and he had several herds. The problem was when the sheep were bedded down for the night, by morning they were never where the herder left them. My job was to ride out and if the herder told me there were lambs missing, I would start cutting the sheep.

I rode between the sheep and let the ewes with lambs go by. Any ewes without a lamb I would turn back, rope, and tie two of their feet together so they could stand but they could not run away. Then I rode back to where that herd had bedded down the night before and look for those missing little lambs. When I found them I roped them and took them to the ewes I had tied up. If a ewe claimed a lamb, I unhobbled her and let her go. If a ewe did not claim a lamb, I left her hobbled and a pickup came out several times a day and picked up those ewes and lambs and returned them to the ranch to be put into those small stalls called day corrals until the ewes claimed the lambs. That is how a herder knows if there are any missing baby lambs and keeps his herds together.

Having to rope those little lambs and ewes, I really perfected my roping skill. I was in the saddle from early morning until dusk. Ross was supposed to feed, water, look after the sheep kept in the day corral, and help form new herds. Instead of doing his job to the best of his ability, he chose to lie on top of the hay and sleep his time away. Ross was the first hand June let go. When Ross was getting ready to leave, he assumed I had been let go too. I told Ross I had not heard anything about leaving. So I went to see June and asked if he was letting me go.

"Hell no. Not if you want to stay. I am keeping you. I am letting Ross go, though," June replied with a grin, because we both knew Ross was pretty lazy.

It was a common practice for the ranchers to help each other. So to keep me busy when things were slow, June loaned me out to work for the Anchor D ranch branding cattle. When the branding was finished, I helped J.R. put in the winter supply of feed called cotton seed cakes.

It was in the middle of winter when I received a letter from Dad asking if I had any extra money I could send him. Tragedy had struck him again. Their house had burned to the ground and the family had lost everything they owned. I immediately went to June and drew what wages I had coming and offered to sell Cherry to him.

"Let me just give you the money you need and you can work it out and keep your horse." June proposed.

June did not want to take Cherry from me. I thought about what June had proposed. I quickly calculated how much time it would take me to pay off that much money. I was not ready to commit myself to stay there for another year, so I told June no. I explained to June that I appreciated his offer, but I would feel better about the money if he took Cherry. So June gave the money to me and I sent as much money to Dad as I could. From the depths of my heart I knew that Cherry would have a good home with June and that made selling him easier.

My daydreams were abruptly ended when a command to come to attention was announced. Another work detail was being formed.

I DID NOT TRUST THE Japanese and I never presumed they would keep their word about anything. I still held hope that an all out rescue was just over the horizon, and I would watch longingly every day for an American armada.

The only news we heard was from the Japanese. They could not wait to rub our noses in every American defeat. When no American assault appeared on the horizon, I began to wonder. Could it be possible that the Japanese were telling us the truth? Could it be possible that the United

States was being beaten? I could not bring myself to believe that. Yet where were our navy, our air force, our ground troops?

Almost three weeks had passed from the day of surrender when we were told we were leaving Wake Island. It was January 12, 1942. We were given a one-hour notice to get ready. I was told to wear warm clothes since it was cold where I was going. That might have been good advice, except I never had any. The only clothes most of us had were fashioned for the tropics. I quickly gathered my few belongings for a trip to God-only-knew-where. We were told to take care of "nature's call" before leaving the barracks.

I had several friends with whom I had worked in the kitchen and they liked me. They tried to convince me to stay with them on Wake Island. They were forced to stay to cook for the hundred or so Americans being kept there.

There was a lot of junk still lying around, and they wanted me to step aside and hide behind some of the junk. They believed the Americans would undoubtedly come very soon and take Wake Island back and they would be liberated. If I went to Japan, it would be months before the war was over and I would be stuck there. None of us thought the war would ever last four years.

When it came time to say goodbye, I almost stayed. I was thinking about it and that little voice deep inside told me, "Do not do it." So I bid my friends a final goodbye and promised to get in touch after the war. They, too, were shot and killed with Al in 1943.

A long list of new rules were passed out to us. Rules that had to be followed when we boarded the ship. We were not to eat more food than we were given and we were not to touch the ship and things like that. The threat of immediate death was always the punishment should we break the rules and their idea of immediate death was to amputate your head. About the only thing we were allowed to do was breathe.

"I thought we were getting too comfortable," I told my friend Ivan Carden.

"Yeah. Here we go again," Carden replied.

I listed just a few of the regulations below. I found some of them very hard to understand. Like a politician's speech with lots of promises if we cooperated and nothing but hardships if we did not. The Japanese wanted us to join them in their Great Imperial prosperous whatever. But then I thought that is how I got here in the first place trying to get prosperous and I did not want any part of it.

A. All prisoners disobeying the following orders will be punished with death.
   1. Those disobeying orders and instructions.
   2. Those showing a motion of antagonism and raising a sign of opposition.

3. Those disordering the regulations by individualism, egoism, thinking only about yourself, rushing for your own goods.
4. Those talking without permission and raising loud voices.
5. Those walking and moving without order.
6. Those carrying unnecessary baggage in embarking.
7. Those resisting mutually.
8. Those touching the boat's materials, wires, electrical lights, tools, switches, etc.
9. Those climbing the ladder without order.
10. Those showing action of running away from the room or boat.
11. Those trying to take more meal than given them.
12. Those using more than two blankets.

B. Since the ship is not well equipped and inside passages being narrow, food being scarce and poor, you will feel uncomfortable during the short time on the ship. Those losing patience and disordering the regulations will be heavily punished for the reason of not being able to escort.

C. Meals will be given two times daily. One bowl only to one prisoner. The prisoners called by the guard will give out the meal as quickly as possible and honestly. The remaining prisoners will stay in their places quietly and wait for their bowl. Those moving from their places, reaching for a bowl without order will be heavily punished. The same orders will be applied in handling bowls after meals.

D. The buckets and cans will be placed at the four corners of the room. Toilet paper will be given. When filled a guard will appoint a prisoner to take the buckets to the center of the room. The buckets will be pulled up by the derrick and emptied overboard. Everyone must cooperate to make the room sanitary. Those being careless will be punished.

E. The Navy of the Great Japanese Empire will not try to punish you all with death. Those obeying all the rules and regulations and believing the action and purpose of the Japanese Navy, cooperating with Japan in constructing the "New order of the Great Asia," which will lead to the world's peace, those will be well treated.

We left the barracks under heavy guard, and we were marched to the baseball field where a mountain of clothing was piled. Everyone was handed a duffle bag and told to fill it up. Some of the clothing was bloody and I assumed it had been removed from dead Americans and Japanese. We stuffed as much as we could into those duffle bags. When the bags were filled to capacity, we were marched about three or four miles to the coast and turned over to the Japanese Navy.

◁ ◁ ◁ ◁ ▷ ▷ ▷ ▷

Chapter Eight

I WAS LOADED ONTO A MOTOR LAUNCH AND TAKEN OUT to a large barge anchored next to the *Nitta Maru*, a former luxury liner that had been converted to a transport ship. I carried the duffle bag on my shoulders as did all the others. I was marched single-file up a long gangplank that led from the launch to the barge. Then I was marched across the barge to another long gangplank that led up to the large cargo doors located on the side of the *Nitta Maru*. The whole process reminded me of what I called a sheep shoot back home on the farm.

From the gangplank I could hear the waves of an indifferent sea lapping against the ship. How I wished I was going home instead of to some unknown destination. We were made to throw the filled duffle bags to the side as we entered the cargo doors. Several Japanese sailors were there to take the duffle bags, and each man was carefully searched and any personal belongings were confiscated never to be seen again. I never saw the duffle bags again, either. I should have known the Japanese would not let us keep anything.

After throwing those duffle bags aside, I was made to run through a gauntlet that ran the full length of a long hallway. Japanese sailors were standing on each side and they were six footers, great big rascals. They looked more like Japanese marines than sailors. They were staggered about twenty feet apart and held bamboo sticks about three feet long and hit you as hard as they could as you ran past. Some tried to hit you with their gun butt or poke you with a bayonet. Not enough to kill you, but enough to maim you and put you in pain. It was like a big game for them to hurt us.

The bottom of the ship was filled first, and since I was in the first large group to be taken aboard, I was made to climb down to the bottom. Because I was at the tail end of that large group, I was seated in the center of the ship very close to the ladder that led to the upper decks. On one hand, being in the center made a much smoother ride than being placed at the bow or stern. And yet on the other, I was always splattered with the urine and fecal matter from the honey buckets when they were pulled topside. There was nothing made easy on the *Nitta Maru*.

It seemed I had passed three decks before finally reaching the bottom, which was thirty-two feet below the water line. There had to have been at least thirty feet of space above me. I calculated there must have been at least six decks above me. There was only about ten feet of space above those decks.

Again we were crowded as cattle in a shipping car on their way to the slaughterhouse. There were wooden slats around the inside of the bottom of the ship to keep the cargo from hitting the outside structure and causing serious damage. There were several grass ropes hanging on those wooden slats. Some of the men made swings out of those grass ropes and sat up in the air until their buttocks went to sleep. Then they would stand for a little while then sit back in their swing again. Actually sitting on those ropes for a long time was very uncomfortable. The only advantage of being up in the air was you had room to move your legs and arms.

We were so crowded together we had to take turns sitting back to back with our arms hugged around our knees so we could make enough room for someone to lie and sleep. We had to do that for hours at a time and it was very exhausting. In spite of my discomfort I would try to grab an elusive wink now and then. It was impossible to get any sound sleep in that position. Those times were long and torturous for me. I found a certain amount of content daydreaming about the past, and my thoughts were about Coley.

WHILE IN ARKANSAS, COLEY, MARRIED a young lady named Rosie Burris. They returned to New Mexico and lived in Hagerman. I was so anxious to see Coley and meet his new bride, I could not think of anything else. I found them living in an old abandoned hotel with broken windows and everything else that goes with vacated buildings. Rosie was cooking on a two-burner Coleman stove, and wooden lug boxes were stacked against the wall for cupboards. They were sleeping on an old dirty mattress that was lying on the floor. Cowboys had better living conditions in the line shacks located in the high country.

Coley was working for fifteen cents an hour on a farm four miles away and walked to and from work everyday. Two days after I arrived I happened to meet Mr. West on the street. He owned a large farm and was looking for help. Mr. West had known Dad for years and he gave me and Coley jobs. He had a vacant house on his farm and he let Coley and his wife move into it.

Coley became foreman and everything started looking up for us. It was not very long until my oldest brother, Red, arrived from Arkansas to join us.

We worked together ten hours a day each making fifteen cents an hour. We hoed cotton, baled alfalfa, or irrigated. Red and I paid three dollars a week to Rosie for board and room and doing our laundry. I had not had things that good for a long time. I had plenty of money and two of my best friends, Red and Coley to go into town with me every Saturday night. The only one other person missing who could have made that time in my life more complete was Skeet.

Red drank quite a bit at the local saloon and in a short time owed the bartender a week's wages. So the next payday Mr. West gave Red a week's wages in advance to pay his bill.

Red paid his bill and drank up another nine dollars worth of liquor. It was getting late and I was tired. I was not paying much attention to Red. He was talking to another cowboy across the room. I motioned to Red that I was leaving and he sort of waved a nonchalant hand of recognition that I took as goodnight. Come Monday morning Red did not show up for work and Mr. West asked me and Coley where Red was. I told him that I left him in the saloon Saturday night and Coley thought Red might be in jail, so Mr. West sent me into town to find him.

I hurried into town and went directly to the bar where I had left Red. The bartender told me that Red took the job of riding the rush string at the Turkey Tracks. The Turkey Tracks was the name given to a large ranch in the area that had a certified brand that looked just like a turkey foot.

I wondered why Red would he do that, and the bartender told me they needed somebody right away and offered him a deal he could not refuse. I returned to the farm to tell Coley and Mr. Wast.

For those who do not know what a rush string is: The larger ranches have lots of horses they never ride and hardly ever feed. Come roundup time they ride those horses until they get weak, then run in another bunch and ride them until they become exhausted. They keep repeating the process, and in many ways it is a cruel procedure for the horses. The horses they use are called the rush string. Those horses get pretty mean and become outlaws and throw most cowboys off. To save the cowboys from serious injury, the ranches hire one man to ride those horses first and calm them down. That is what Red hired out to do.

The next week when payday rolled around, I told Mr. West to keep my wages of nine dollars for what Red owed him. Red never did pay me back. As far as I know that is the only debt he never paid because Red was as honest as they come. A bit rough and tough as leather, but honest. Still that nine dollars is one bill Red never paid.

"Nine dollars," I repeated. At that time in my life nine dollars was quite a bit of money. If only I could see Red again just to tell him the nine dollars was not important and to just forget it. I was brought back to the present by the sheer feeling of misery.

WE WERE ALL VERY MUCH mistreated on the *Nitta Maru,* and I was troubled again about the uncertainty of our immediate future. When I was not thinking about the past, I tried to convince myself I was on a ship sailing for Honolulu. I finally had to stop myself from thinking about anything except surviving. In the darkness I could not hold back the silent tears any longer. Tears that longed to fall ever since our forces had to surrender.

We were given two five-gallon cans with the tops cut off to relieve ourselves and there was just enough light to find our way to the cans. When the cans were filled the prisoners above us would pull the cans up by grass ropes. The cans would sway and hit the side of the ship, spilling their contents over us. The scene was one of a slave ship in the mid-1800s with the same results you would expect in that type of atmosphere. Stench, nausea, dysentery, and suffocation.

I sat for what seemed like hours and listened while the decks above were being filled. Finally the sound of marching feet, cries of agony, and shouts of orders gave way to the sound of the anchor chain being pulled up. The noise reverberated throughout the bottom of the ship and the powerful propellers began churning heavily to get the ship underway. The noise was deafening for us at the bottom. There were times when that ship sounded as if it was falling apart and it was very scary.

I could feel the giant swells beneath my feet as the ship finally got on the way. During the first few hours we were given a granite bowl to hold our ration of food and were told if anyone was caught trying to take extra food rations, he would be shot. They never gave us any utensils, chopsticks, or anything to eat with. We were given one cup of rice gruel in the morning and evening and one cup of water to drink at each meal. Sometime the rice had seaweed in it. The rice was so runny we did not need any utensils—we just drank it. I closed my eyes when I ate. If there was anything unpleasant to see in that rice, I did not want to know it. I fortified myself with whatever strength I could gather to survive no matter what. I tried to think of more happier days to take my mind away from all the suffering and pain I was forced to endure. I could not help but smile when I thought about the time Coley and I decided to go into the rabbit-hunting business.

COLEY AND HIS WIFE SEPARATED and Rosie returned to Arkansas. Coley and I kept hearing how much money there was to be made hunting cotton-tail rabbits, so we decided to try it. The going rate for rabbits was one dollar a dozen if they were shot in the head. If the rabbits were shot anywhere else other than the head, we received only sixty cents a dozen. It was important to be a good shot.

Coley and I needed transportation and decided to get a truck. Coley found an old Model T that had a cute little bed on the back, so Coley bought it for ten dollars. We were overjoyed. All I knew about the Model T was you had to crank it to start it. I cranked until I thought my arm was going to fall off and that old hunk of junk would not start. I was pretty disgusted when Coley wanted to know what the problem was.

"That old thing is dead. I cannot of get it started," I replied.

Coley walked to the driver's side, looked in and reached down and set the emergency brake so the pickup would not run over you when you cranked it. Then he walked to the front and cranked it. The old Model T started on the first turn. I felt a little foolish for not thinking to do that and appreciated Coley not saying anything about my incompetence.

We loaded the car with all our belongings. Bed rolls, cooking utensils and of course, the reliable Coleman stove. We each bought a .22 pump rifle and ammunition in a box the size of a dynamite box. We also bought extra gas and limited groceries since we planned to have rabbit for dinner every night. When we had everything we felt was needed, we set out to hunt rabbits. We left town on a high level of self-satisfaction. We were sure we would triple our investment within the first week.

The country across the Pecos River was very sandy and perfect cotton-tail rabbit country. At that time paved roads had not yet come to many parts of New Mexico, and we were on one of the worst roads I had ever been on. We had traveled several miles down a deserted, hole-ridden road that was anything but smooth. I thought my bones were gonna shake loose. It was almost dark and we were miles from town when the front wheel came off. The axel dropped down and hit the ground with such a force that the groceries, gas, ammunition and everything we had piled in back was thrown out into the sand.

That happened so suddenly that by the time Coley and I collected our thoughts and checked out what had happened, it was too dark to find everything. We used a big box of matches looking for wheel parts. We finally gave up looking for them and decided to make camp for the night and take care of everything in the morning.

Around eleven o'clock we saw headlights coming toward us. We could not believe our good fortune because I would bet there were not three cars a week that traveled that road. The man stopped and gave us a ride into town. It was in the wee hours of the morning when Coley awakened the man at a garage to ask him if he had a wheel bearing for a Model T. He did not have one; however, he had one for a Chevrolet. Coley was sure he could make it fit the axel of the Model T, so we bought it. The man who gave us a lift into town was pretty nice and drove us back to the Model T. He wished us good luck and drove away.

The next morning I fixed fried potatoes for breakfast while Coley organized the wheel parts. We worked like hell getting that Model T back together. Since the Chevrolet bearing on the hub was the wrong size, the wheel wobbled but not so much that Coley worried about having it fixed properly before continuing the hunting trip. We probably should have headed toward town, but we did not.

Coley and I piled everything back into the Model T and drove away just as if we had good sense. Of course we could not travel very fast with that wobbly wheel, and I will bet we were not three miles from where the wheel fell off when we pulled over and set up camp.

I saw rabbits running in every direction and knew we were in a good area. I was confident we were going to have a great day. Needless to say that shooting a rabbit in the head while the rabbit was running at top speed, darting in and out of mesquite bushes, was a challenge indeed.

Coley and I wore a big belt with a hook on it. We would hang the rabbit's legs over that hook and our pant legs would get stiff from the knees down when the rabbit's blood dried.

We walked for miles that first day and had killed about ten or twelve rabbits. Our high level of self-satisfaction was rapidly evaporating. We returned to camp very disappointed. The next day we did a little better. By the end of the week our marksmanship had improved immensely.

In spite of the disappointments and the extra work, Coley and I did pretty well the first two or three weeks. We shot a lot of rabbits, but very few were shot in the head and we did not make as much money as we were hoping for. We barely covered our initial investment. I am not talking about big money. If Coley and I had thirty dollars between us at one time, we would have been rich.

Another problem that became very obvious was the number of men hunting rabbits. Not only for the fur, but for food for their families, and the rabbits were getting scarce. Everyone thought there was an endless supply of rabbits so there were not any limits on how many you could kill.

Coley and I had to travel farther and farther away to find any rabbits. We had to go at least sixty miles away from the nearest town. That extra forty cents a dozen offered for rabbits shot in the head sure improved our aim. Coley and I figured we did not need as many rabbits if we were paid a dollar a dozen, and that alone was the real incentive for becoming superb marksmen.

Then came the day the god of misfortune smiled down on us. Coley ran over a sand hill and without any warning the wheels on that old Model T turned to a sharp right and Coley lost control. The Model T went through a homesteader's fence. The posts had been buried in shallow sand and were not very close together. When the Model T hit that wire fence, the impact pulled the posts down and every post began to fall over just like standing dominoes. Coley backed up and shook his head in disgust and yelled, "Dammit."

Although it was not a very good fence, it was the only fence the homesteader could afford and it was up to Coley and I to restore it.

The homesteader came out to see if we were hurt. He turned out to be an all right kind of fellow and the three of us worked until sunset repairing that fence. When we finally finished, Coley and I decided to drive to

Velma's and spend the night. Dallas was not home and Velma was glad to see us. She lived a lonely existence and loved having company.

The following morning Coley and I set out early. With every trip we had to travel farther and farther out of town to find any rabbits, and it was getting to be winter. Although there had not been any bad storms to hit the area as of yet, we knew it was only a matter of time.

We were about seventy miles out of town when the wind began to blow. Threatening dark clouds moved over us. It was obvious a rainstorm was coming. We decided we had better make camp and do what little hunting we could before the storm hit. Coley carried a tarp just in case of rain. Our bedrolls were just a couple of old quilts and blankets. We did not have sleeping bags then.

The hunting was not very good and the weather was even worse, although the hunt was not all in vain. I shot a coyote and I would probably get anywhere from three to five dollars for the hide. The weather turned real ugly and it began raining. The tarp that Coley had was full of holes and leaked. We were anything but comfortable.

During the night the temperature plummeted and we thought we were going to freeze to death before morning. We picked up our bedrolls and literally threw our things into the back of the pickup. We drove to Velma's again to dry out and spend the night. Coley and I agreed that hunting rabbits was not a profitable business and more trouble than it was worth. We quit the rabbit business for good with less money than when we started. "Money," I whispered to myself, "the root of all evil." Again the word *money* brought about bitter thoughts.

SUDDENLY THE SHIP TURNED SHARPLY throwing all of us off balance. The ship was zig-zagging wildly and rolling with the swells. I wondered what was going on. That is when I heard the unmistakable high pitch of torpedoes whizz by us. I thought of the many times I had prayed to be rescued and help finally arrives when I am trapped in the bowels of that ship.

I knew if we were hit by torpedoes, those of us at the bottom would not have a chance in hell of escaping. I did not want to go to a watery grave and spend an eternity in Davy Jones's locker. I was terrified along with all the others. I silently prayed and I caught myself holding my breath I was so scared. I broke out in another cold sweat over that incident.

The *Nitta Maru* was known as one of the Japanese silk ships. It could travel over thirty knots an hour, and the *Nitta Maru* simply outran the submarine. Even under such miserable conditions, life was precious and although we wanted the Japanese to pay for their transgressions, we did not want to go down under such circumstances. It is one thing to go down fighting and another to have to sit and have your life taken without being able to do anything about it. I was greatly relieved when the torpedoes missed us; for that, I was extremely thankful.

Soon after that, several men became seasick and could not make it to the cans. Many of the men had dysentery and they could not make it to the cans, either. Within a few hours the stench was overwhelming. Not only that, it was hot as hell down in the bottom of that ship and many of the men began tossing their clothes aside. The heat made us so thirsty we would have drunk sea water if we could have gotten to it.

It was not very long until the beatings started, and they seemed to go on all the time somewhere on that ship. The Japanese guards got their pleasure from beating us for absolutely nothing. It was almost like a sporting event for them. It did not take us long to realize we were sailing on a ship from hell.

When the captain read the name Nokanishni on the list of prisoners, he had Nokanishni brought up from the hole. When the Japanese captain could not convert him, the Japanese sailors beat him severely and threw him back into the hole. Poor Nokanishni. He had barely recovered from the beatings he had received on Wake Island, and he was made to go through it all over again. He told us if he survived the war, he was going to change his name to Jones. Nokanishni had quite a sense of humor and I liked him.

Being at the bottom of the ship, I could not tell whether it was night or day. I had only my internal clock and the changing of the guard to let me know when a day had passed. Day after day, night after night, I had to sit until my buttocks felt like there was no life there anymore. My whole body was weary and aching from the uncomfortable positions.

Time was slow in passing and having nothing to do was even more exhausting. Yet I tried keeping positive thoughts about the future. Many times I would retreat into the world of my daydreams in an attempt to escape an intolerable situation. The daydreams became so real that nothing existed around me, and I would abruptly be brought to reality by the men reminding me it was time to change positions. Time to turn the other cheek, so to speak.

Chapter Nine

NONE OF US KNEW WHERE WE WERE GOING. There was not a man who did not speculate and wonder what was to become of us. The farther north we sailed, the colder the weather became and we started freezing down in that hole. The men quickly put all their clothes back on. No matter how cold we became, no blankets were offered by the Japanese. Once more I prayed to be rescued, but not by a submarine's torpedoes.

After six long, difficult days, we anchored off Japan. A few men were brought up on deck with a few American officers who were photographed and questioned by reporters for propaganda. That is when I learned we were anchored off Yokohama. After the Japanese had taken their pictures, eight officers and a dozen men were taken off ship to be questioned. All of us worried for their safety, especially the noncoms. Up until then the officers of Wake Island were always treated better than the enlisted men and the civilians. When they never returned we thought they too had been killed but later the scuttlebutt drifted down to us that they had been put in a POW camp in Japan.

From Yokohama, we sailed to China. We had not been out to sea very long when scuttlebutt came down that five men had been chosen at random and taken topside and beheaded. Lieutenant Toshio Saito, commander of the guards, ordered five of his men to use their sabers and behead those five Americans and mutilate the bodies before throwing them overboard. None of us could understand the reason for doing such a dastardly deed since no one knew what they had done. I thought since the Japanese used fear to control, killing those men was probably done to keep order. I could not understand why they had to be so brutal when we were already so scared it was sickening.

The men's names were Seaman First Class John W. Lambert, Seaman Second Class Theodore D. Franklin, Seaman Second Class Roy J. Gonzales, Master Sergeant Earl Raymond Hannum, and Technical Sergeant William Bailey.

I never knew why those five brave men were executed until much later. An interpreter told us that they were chosen to be the representatives of all American soldiers and murdered for revenge because the Americans had killed so many of the Imperial troops on Wake Island. When I heard that explanation it sent a powerful message to me, and I am sure it was not the message our captors intended. By executing those five brave men, by showing their need for revenge, they unmeaningly gave a great testimony to just how much we had damaged their Imperial ego.

After the war, four of the five executioners were sentenced to life in prison. The fifth was acquitted. However, the men were paroled nine years later. Saito was never apprehended.

About six days later, the *Nitta Maru* docked at Woo Sung. We were told we were leaving the ship. I had been in a sitting position so long my legs and feet felt numb. When I stood the prickles in my feet were rather unpleasant. The thought occurred to me that at least part of my anatomy had gotten some sleep.

I was weak from immobility and the lack of food. I had lost some of my strength and climbing that ladder was painfully difficult; I had to use all the strength I could gather. When I finally reached an outside deck, I felt faint. It was being out in the open and able to breathe fresh air again that revitalized me a little. Seeing the sky and having fresh air was wonderful beyond words. Even though the sky was filled with dark angry storm clouds, it looked beautiful to me.

Before we were allowed to disembark, we had to run through big troughs about two feet long, and about knee high. They had about four inches of what looked like potash. I guess it was to delouse us or something, or maybe it was for athlete's foot. I was never told what it was and I could not understand how four inches of anything could delouse us all over.

When we reached the outside there were eighteen inches of snow on the ground and it was colder than dry ice. We were not dressed for snow in any way. We were wearing island clothes and not very many of those.

The Japanese lined us up and told us through the interpreter that we had to march about four miles to a prison camp located about twelve miles out of Shanghai. Should anyone fall he would be shot. Since the group I was with had been located at the bottom of the *Nitta Maru*, we were the last ones to leave the ship, so we brought up the rear. There must have been men strung out ahead of us for at least two miles.

We were double-timed through an area with many canals. Many Chinese families lived on houseboats called sampans and they never left those canals. The Chinese were fixing their supper and I was so hungry that the aroma of food cooking was almost more than I could take. Not being able to get to it was sheer torture.

We were double-timed six abreast until we came to a small bridge and we had to break the ranks to four. Naturally that slowed the column. The Japanese soldiers who thought we were not moving fast enough and who could not speak English would gruffly vocalize, "Ugh, ugh," and cruelly poke us with their bayonets. The Japanese bayonets were much longer than the American bayonets. There were several bridges we had to cross along the way, and no matter what the obstacle, we dared not slow our pace.

At least doing double-time made you sweat and kept you from freezing to death. So we kept moving. I breathed a sigh of thankfulness after every deterrent that I made it without being stuck or killed. I counted my blessings when I had escaped the attention of the Japanese soldiers.

The situation sparked memories and I thought of the day Coley sold that old wobbly wheeled Model T to Dallas for a guitar and another .22 rifle. I remembered what a sad picture we must have made; yet, unlike my present circumstances, there were laughs with every disaster.

DALLAS COULD NOT WAIT TO drive it and offered to take us into town, which was sixty miles away. Coley wanted to show Dallas how to use all the gears before getting behind the wheel and Dallas reluctantly agreed.

You can imagine what we looked like with about thirty dozen dead rabbits, all our belongings, bed rolls, cooking utensils, and the four of us crowded together in that single seated Model T with its wobbly wheel. We were laughing and making jokes as if we did not have a care in the world.

We had only traveled about six miles when Dallas insisted on getting behind the wheel. Coley was hesitant to let Dallas drive, but Dallas was adamant and yelled, "It is my car and I am going to drive." Dallas was like a little kid with a new toy. He slid under the wheel and raced the motor. Dallas wanted to know just what that old car could do.

"I would not race the motor like that Dallas. You cannot make a track star out of a ninety-year-old man," Coley advised, wanting Dallas to realize the car was far from being new. But Dallas would not listen and chose to ignore Coley completely. He came to a pretty good-sized patch of thick sand and raced the motor real hard and fast. The piston busted and blew clear out from under the hood. We were still miles away from the highway.

I looked up at the horizon and saw a Blue Norther coming. For those who do not know what a Blue Norther is: You look north and you can see a thin blue streak just over the horizon. The closer it gets, the higher up in the air the blue streak. It is always a big, powerful wind that is bitter cold followed by snow or icy rains.

Fortunately we were less than two miles from a line camp. The ranches were so big that they built small one-room shacks across certain areas so the cowboys would have good shelter while looking after the cattle. Those shacks were called line camps.

We grabbed our guns and Coley carried his guitar. We hurried to that line camp. At least we would be out of the weather. Although most doors had locks on them, they were seldom used in those days.

That line camp was furnished with a bedstead and mattress, a cook stove, and some wood. There was a can of bacon grease on the stove and upon a shelf flour, salt, a box of matches, and a deck of cards. Dallas built a fire and Coley made biscuits and fixed gravy.

To pass the time we played poker. At first we played for matches. Then we played for the rabbits. To this day Coley claims he wound up with all the matches and I got all the rabbits. It was really immaterial because when I sold the rabbits there was no way I would keep all the money, especially after Coley and I had worked so hard getting them.

The next morning the storm had passed and we returned to the Model T to gather our paraphernalia, including the rabbits. Dallas told us goodbye at the Model T and wished us good luck. Coley and I still had miles to walk before reaching the highway. As we walked away, I turned to wave a final goodbye to Dallas, but he did not see me. He had his head lowered in disgust as he began walking home in the other direction.

Coley and I sat on the side of the highway with that mountain of stuff, which was everything we owned. Coley looked disgusted and expressed his feelings when he said, "Nobody is ever going to stop and pick us up with this load."

"I cannot believe that. Who would have thought a car would have come and picked us up on that lonely road in the middle of the night when that wheel fell off," I remanded him.

"We will probably grow old by the side of the road," Coley replied and then added, "That sounds like a good verse to me for a song," and Coley began picking his guitar.

God must have been looking after us, for lo and behold, the first vehicle to come along was a truck pulling a homemade open-horse trailer that was made out of two-by-fours. The man stopped and yelled, "You can ride in the trailer."

We were so thankful for the lift we carelessly tossed our stuff into the trailer. Without any protection it is a wonder Coley and I did not freeze to death as we breezed down the road in that open trailer with a cold wind blowing directly on us.

When we reached Roswell, I happened to see June Tulk on the street and he insisted I go home with him. Coley urged me to go with June. He explained he wanted to find Rosie and try to patch things up, and it would be much easier for him knowing I was safely tucked in for the winter. Like an obedient little brother, I automatically agreed to whatever Coley told me to do and I went home with June.

I was glad to see my horse Cherry. June had taken real good care of him. In fact Cherry was getting fat. I suspected he had not been ridden for awhile. I decided the first day the weather permitted I would give Cherry some much needed exercise.

My daydream was interrupted by the most unpleasant odor that filled the air and was so foul it offended my nose to the point I could not think of anything but my present circumstances.

WE TRAVERSED AN AREA WHERE there were many gardens. I would be going along and I would smell something that smelled like the man next to me had soiled himself. So I would speed up a little to get away from him. When I caught up with the next guy he to smelled the same way. The foul odor seemed to permeate the area. That is when I noticed several Chinese with dippers throwing fecal matter out of buckets onto the plants. They used human waste to fertilize their gardens and that was the foul odor I had been smelling.

I am sure the Japanese lied when they told us that we had only four miles to march to the prison camp. Maybe as the crow flies, but it felt more like ten or twelve miles. I was exhausted by the time I arrived there and glad, too, because I did not know how much further I could have gone.

The prison camp was an old Chinese cavalry camp. There were twelve barracks, a cook shack, sheds, and corrals for the horses that were no longer there. The camp was surrounded with an electrical fence that carried twenty-three thousand volts. It was instant electrocution to touch it.

When we arrived it was dark and it had started snowing. It was getting along towards the end of January by then. I had lost track of time. They had Chinese preparing the barracks for us and they were not finished, so we were put in the corrals until the barracks were ready. It was pretty cold out there in those corrals. It was around ten o'clock at night before we were allowed to enter the barracks and there were so many of us we filled seven of them.

The barracks were very long with approximately a four-foot-wide pathway down the middle. U-shaped opened cubicles were built on each side of that pathway and held nine men. A platform had been built across each cubical about fourteen inches from the floor and six feet in length. The platform was for sleeping.

We were allowed twenty inches each in width to lie and sleep on that platform, without any extra room to turn over whatsoever. We had to sleep like a room full of mummies but not nearly as comfortable. Nonetheless, we cooperated with each other and endured whatever the Japanese did to us.

A shelf was built above the platform extending the full length. That shelf was built with twenty-inch sections so we each had a little box in which to put our personal items, except we did not have any personal items. All we had was a little sack the Japanese had given us that contained a rice bowl, a tiny tea cup, and a glass spoon. The kind you see in every Chinese restaurant.

We were all cold and starving. Considering how we were treated on the *Nitta Maru* imagine our surprise when the most delicious hot curry stew was given to us with a big bowl of rice on the side. The stew had big hunks of meat in it, and the Japanese were very generous with the servings. I was so happy over getting something good to eat for a change I got carried away and I yelled, "Bring on the girls and I will sign up with this outfit."

That remark brought about several lighthearted smiles from my companions, but everyone was afraid to laugh out loud. Laughter might be misunderstood so we had to be very careful. Actually I spoke out of turn without thinking. There was no way I would join the Japanese in anything. Thank God neither my friends nor the guards took offense. An interpreter told us that that POW camp was a modern model camp. I worried about that. When the Japanese began being good to us there had to be a reason, and I wondered what they were up to.

Later we were given two blankets and told if we tried to take someone else's blanket or take more than two, we would be shot. Unfortunately the blankets had been washed and they were still damp, but at least they were clean. I welcomed the chance to lie down and stretch my legs to full length. Even if the bed was hard, just to at last close my eyes and have peaceful rest was welcoming indeed. It seemed too good to be true.

Once I was settled with my eyes closed, I mentally would catch a ship to Hawaii, then I catch another ship to San Francisco. I would get off the ship in San Francisco and my brothers would be there to greet me. We would drive home to Paskenta. My daydreams were so real I could feel the gangplank beneath my feet. I would fall asleep praying that those daydreams would someday come true. Until then sleep was a chance to escape, a chance to dream of my first trip to California.

AFTER COLEY AND I SPLIT UP, Coley went to Arkansas and left me with June Tulk. As days will, those of that winter with June Tulk slipped by. I rode Cherry over to see Russ, only to find that he was not home. His brother Jay answered the door and invited me in. Jay was two years older than me and living at home because he was out of work.

We talked about this and that, and then Jay asked me if lambing had started yet. I hesitated saying anything about June needing help since I knew June would never hire Russ again. I did not want to let Jay know his brother was lazy. I tried to be as diplomatic as I could when I told Jay I would ask June but not to expect anything.

When I returned to the ranch and asked June about giving Jay Ledbetter a job, June was reluctant to commit himself and asked if Jay was related to Russ. I told him Jay was his brother, but I thought he would be a better worker. June took my word and told me to have Jay come see him, and that is how Jay got a job with June. I was so glad when Jay did not let me or June down. He was a good worker and June was pleased. It was not long before Jay and I became close buddies.

A man named Mike McLennan was the cook at the ranch. Every night around the supper table in the cook-shack, the men talked about their travels and what they had done. One of the favorite subjects, other than work and women, was California. The men told endless stories about California. Those stories captured the imaginations of Mike, Jay, and me. We had heard so many times what a beautiful state California was, so we decided when lambing was over, we would go there and see that paradise for ourselves.

Soon as lambing was finished, Mike, Jay, and I quit. June wished us good fortune on our venture. I almost cried when I told Cherry goodbye again. I still held hope of buying Cherry back someday.

Mike had the cutest little 1926 Model T that was in showroom condition. The three of us packed our bedrolls, put a few dishes and pans in that little box on back of the car and headed west. Just talking about California seemed to open a magical door to an adventure to paradise. We were anxious to get there as soon as possible, but you could not travel very fast in a Model T. If you drove a steady forty miles an hour, you were wheeling.

Every evening before sunset we pulled over and made camp, cooking our supper over a campfire. When we reached Carrizozo, another man who had his family camped by another bush or two up the road came over to visit. He told us it was no use going to California. The pay was only twenty-five cents an hour. Jay and I looked at each other knowingly, because where we came from the hourly wage was only fifteen cents. Even the big ranches only paid one dollar a day and board and you had to work ten-hour days. Even the top hands never made more than forty-five dollars a month and board, so twenty-five cents an hour sounded pretty good. Jay and I wanted to break camp right then and head for California. But it was Mike's car and he was driving and wanted to sleep. From that moment on, Jay and I could hardly wait to reach the Golden State.

Before we reached Buckeye, Arizona, Mike's car broke down. We stopped at a local tavern to cool off. Mike did not have as much money as Jay and I had. To keep from spending what money he had, Mike started patting his stomach and his legs in a rhythmic beat. It made quite a unique sound and a few beer drinkers in the bar liked hearing it and bought several beers for Mike. Entertainment of any kind was welcomed around Buckeye.

Mike kept drinking and patting his stomach until he could hardly stand. Jay and I decided it was time to leave. Mike told everyone in the bar that we were on our way to California to look for work. The men in the bar told us workers were needed chopping cotton for fifteen cents an hour. No way was I going to stay. Nonetheless, Mike wanted to remain and work in the cotton fields for awhile. Jay and I told Mike goodbye and wished him well.

Jay and I grabbed our bedroll and a suitcase and we walked to the bus depot. We bought tickets to Bakersfield, California. I do not know why we chose Bakersfield; we just did. It was two o'clock in the morning when the bus pulled into Bakersfield. The night was almost over so we did not want to spend any money for a hotel room. Since we were in a town that was strange to us, we decided to sit inside that deserted bus depot until morning.

Jay spied a newspaper lying on a seat and grabbed it. He read that workers were needed picking up potatoes in Shafter, wherever that was in that unfamiliar land. Waiting for daylight was tiring and Jay and I fell asleep in the depot. We were awakened by an employee of the bus depot who told us we could not sleep there and asked us to leave. We gathered our things and walked across the street. We went behind a service station where we were out of sight from everyone and laid out our bedrolls. Jay and I fell fast asleep.

With the coming of full daylight, I was very disappointed in the area. In my mind I had pictured big trees and rushing rivers everywhere and nothing like that was in sight. Only dry gritlike sandy soil without any trees lay before us. Very much like that rabbit eaten land in New Mexico. In the distance were dry barren foothills. Jay must have been thinking the same thing because he told me they would have to pay him twenty-five cents an hour to get him to stay there.

The attendant at the service station drew a map for us to Shafter. Jay and I started walking in that direction. Luck was with us when we got a ride to Shafter. When I asked about a job we were put to work right away swamping on a potato truck.

The company we worked for supplied nice tents on wooden platforms for its workers. There were so many tents it looked like an army camp of sorts. There was only one tent platform left and it did not have a tent. Jay and I had to live in the open without any privacy whatsoever. It was not long before Jay and I knew all our neighbors living as we did. At least we would not be sleeping in that gritlike dirt that seemed to get into everything—even between your teeth.

When I complained to one neighbor about how disappointed I was in California, he told me not to judge the state by the area around Bakersfield. He was a camera bug and had pictures of the redwoods, the beautiful mountains, lakes, rivers, and the sandy beaches by the mile along the ocean. After looking at those pictures, as far as I was concerned, everything worth seeing (other than the ocean beaches and Hollywood) was located in northern California.

Just when I was so deep within my thoughts that I swore could smell orange blossoms, I was brought to reality by someone crying in pain or wanting me to move over.

I WAS ALREADY CRUNCHED UP like an accordion. With us being so crowded together, I felt like a hot dog crammed tightly between two buns. My bones felt like rigor mortis had set in. Although it was wonderful to be able to stretch out to full length, having to lie in one position for hour after hour was anything but comfortable. Again I wondered how long I could last under such circumstances.

Chapter Ten

WITH THE COMING OF DAYLIGHT I GOT A GOOD LOOK at my new surroundings. Even though the countryside was under a new blanket of snow it looked marshy and I was very disappointed. I thought it looked better at night. The darkness had covered the unattractiveness of the area.

Guard towers loomed high over us at all four corners of the camp. There was a large, square, wooden water tower located next to the kitchen facilities. The camp was dependent on that old leaky tower for all its water, and even then all the water in China had to be boiled before it was safe to drink.

On the outside of the electric fence was a brick road, and across the road was another electric fence atop a brick wall that surrounded the Japanese guards' barracks. In between those fences was the kitchen.

We were allowed to have a little radio that received only one station and was controlled by the Japanese. We hungered for any kernel of news about the war, so when the Japanese let a few Chinese inside the compound everyday to clean the barracks and honey pots, we tried our best to extract truthful information from them. But they could not understand one word of English. We could not even get our point across with charades. Either they played stupid or just would not answer. After all, the Chinese lived under the gun and were very afraid to do anything wrong. Or maybe we just were not that good at pantomiming.

The only news we ever heard was given to us by the Japanese. With every triumph they strutted around like peacocks and could not wait to trumpet their victories. Our morale sank a little lower with every announcement.

We were also allowed a piece of paper and pencil once in awhile to write letters, but I did not believe the letters ever left Japan. We had one man in camp who was a talented artist, and he began drawing pictures of the conditions. Had he been caught he surely would have been executed. He hid his drawings inside tubes of shaving cream. Those drawings survived many inspections and were never found.

Poor Nokanishni. As soon as the Japanese guards read his name he would be taken and interrogated. When they could not change him to their way of thinking, the guards beat him. Then every three weeks the guards changed and Nokanishni would get beaten some more by the new guards trying to convert him.

During the days to follow, the Japanese took our identities by giving us a number. We were no longer people, just numbers. That was their way to demoralize us even more than we already were. Work parties were organized, and although we had to work hard, it was not slave driving. For that I was thankful.

There were a few men in the barracks who knew electronics. They were chosen to work on the Japanese communication equipment. It was not very long until American ingenuity manifested itself. Little by little they managed to steal a scrap of copper wire here and a small part there. They wanted to build a radio we could send and receive on. It would take them many months to gather all the parts they needed. Everyone in our barracks was well aware if the Japanese ever discovered what the men were doing, the punishment would be severe for all of us. We could even face being executed. However, their efforts brought us closer and gave us purpose. We derived great pleasure having something so forbidden and hidden right under the noses of our enemy.

The weather turned real ugly and the temperatures plummeted to way below zero. Icicles formed around that leaky water tower until it was completely covered and frozen over from top to bottom. About forty feet high, eight or nine square feet of solid ice. It was quite a spectacle to behold.

We started missing meals because the water supply had frozen over and there was not any water for cooking. We were given water that had not been boiled and all of us suffered from dysentery. Everyone's health began to deteriorate, and we were steadily losing weight. Nonetheless, we were still expected to work every day. For a model camp, everyday things began getting worse.

We were allowed about a gallon of coallike briquets every two weeks to keep the barracks warm. So needless to say we were always on the lookout for any wood we could burn. Since that was not nearly enough heat, we had to keep moving to keep from freezing to death.

I was so cold it brought back bitter memories of when I was a kid and homeless in the winter. I remembered the time I came to a cotton field that had been picked and I made what I thought would be a nice bed from the bales of cotton, and it did not work. I tried to stop thinking about the bad times and tried remembering the good. My mind kept wondering about days gone by. I came to the conclusion I would rather be homeless in America than the richest man in any other country.

The shoes I had were pretty worn out with holes in them and my feet were frostbitten. I had chill blains so bad every step was painful. Because of that I would suffer with bad feet for the rest of my life. Chill blains was what we called frostbitten feet. The Japanese issued us wooden cloglike shoes. They were just a one-inch board with a cloth strap across it. We called them "go aheads," because you could not walk backwards without your feet coming out of them. For those who had material, they wrapped their feet. But material of any kind was hard to come by, so most everyone suffered with frost bite.

When you walked across the barracks floor, those wooden clogs made a sound all their own. The back of the shoe would hit your heel making a dull flapping sound while the wood sole hitting the wood floors would make a clacking sound. With all the men having to pace up and down to keep warm the sound of flapping and clacking was going on night and day through those barracks halls.

Rumbles of discontent could be heard coming from the men. They complained about the conditions and wished we could be transferred to another camp. They thought no camp could be as bad as the one we were in. I disagreed with them—I knew things could be worse. My life had always been a little rough and I probably had lived through tougher times than most of the men, so in spite of the bad living conditions at least we were inside and being fed. I counted my blessings and told stories about what had happened to me while in California with Jay.

JAY AND I HAD WORKED a month in Shafter when Jay began getting homesick. I wanted to see northern California before leaving; however, I could not convince Jay. He wanted to return home, back to New Mexico. Since we vowed to stay together on that trip, I did not press it. I knew I would be back again someday. Although I told Jay before we left we should at least see Hollywood, and Jay agreed.

When Jay and I drew our wages I will never forget, we had the same amount of money, fifteen dollars and thirty-five cents. We gave our cooking utensils and groceries to a man for a ride to the railroad depot in Bakersfield. Jay and I decided we did not want to carry our bedrolls and suitcases around Hollywood, so we sent them by freight to Hagerman, New Mexico.

Jay and I caught a freight train going to Los Angeles. The train traveled east of Bakersfield toward Mojave and made a big half circle going through several little desert towns before coming back into Los Angeles. The train stopped at Barstow, and Jay and I jumped off and bought some canned sardines. We sat on an old train platform out in the hot sun and ate them.

The train left the yard about dark heading for Pasadena. Jay and I jumped on an empty box car and Jay complained that he did not feel good. In a few minutes he became real sick and passed out. I could not revive him no matter what I tried. I was scared to death. There was no one around to help, and it would not do any good to stop the train out in the middle of nowhere and try to find someone to save him. I truly thought Jay was going to die before I could get him any help.

I worried about the consequences of having a dead man on my hands. I was a long way from home and I did not know anybody. I was concerned that the authorities might think I killed him. I had heard of things like that happening. I stayed awake all through the dark hours of the night in sleepless misery worrying how to get Jay to a doctor as soon as the train pulled into a town.

About daylight Jay regained consciousness and the joy an relief I felt was almost overwhelming. I could not believe it when I started getting sick. Fortunately, I did not become as ill as Jay. That is when we determined those canned sardines we had in Barstow must have been tainted.

We jumped off the train at Pasadena. We were afraid we might end up in jail if we were caught riding a freight train through the train yards of Los Angeles. We ask a man how to get to Hollywood and he told us to catch a streetcar.

"How do we catch one of those streetcars? Jay asked, since neither of us had never seen one let alone ride one. I know that sounds ridiculous since we were riding freight trains and we did not know how to catch a streetcar.

The man could see by our Stetson hats, our handmade cowboy boots, and western attire that we were out-of-towners. Where Jay and I came from you could wear rags and as long you wore a Stetson and had handmade cowboy boots you were dressed up. At that time handmade boots cost forty-five dollars and that was over a month' wages for most men.

The man turned out to be a nice fellow and told us what streetcar to take to reach Hollywood. He instructed us to be sure and have our dime out and in hand to pay the fare. He also informed us to be sure and ask for a transfer. That way we could get back on the streetcar without paying another dime and ride clear to Long Beach. Jay and I did exactly what he told us to do and we asked the streetcar driver for transfers. When we reached Hollywood we got off and looked the town over pretty good. I do not know how to explain what I did next without sounding foolish. I always liked good clothes and I never had any. I saw a sign, TAILOR-MADE SUITS. I went in and the tailor measured me up one side and down the other. I paid five dollars down on a suit that was going to cost me fifteen dollars, and fifteen dollars was all the money I had in the world And here I am on the bum riding freight trains and planned to leave the area that day. That was about the dumbest thing I have ever pulled. I never did return to pick up that suit.

I was real impressed with the fruit orchards in the area. At last I saw the abundance of fruit that flowed from the horn of plenty that California was famous for growing.

When we left the area, Jay and I thought we could walk on any street going east and reach the highway going to Yuma. We walked and walked and walked and never reached the edge of town. We finally grew tired of walking and not getting anywhere, so we decided to catch a streetcar. The streetcars kept passing us by without stopping. We could not figure out why the streetcars would not stop. Jay thought it was because we were wearing cowboy hats, since he noticed the men in the area did not wear hats. So we took our hats off and the streetcars still passed us by. We found out we were on the wrong side of the street. I felt so foolish at that point I thought we should get out of town as fast as possible.

Jay and I started walking east again. We walked and walked until finally a truck driver stopped and took us almost to Yuma. It was a little after sunup when the truck driver let us off. The country looked like no-man's-land. No trees, no shade, no water, and no civilization. Standing out in the blinding heat of the noonday sun was almost more than we could take, and it kept getting hotter.

We stood on that highway from sunup until one in the afternoon in the full sun without one car even slowing down to help us. We were thirsty and needed to find some shade. We had walked about a mile when at last a car stopped and offered us a ride if we would buy him some gas in Yuma. He could see we were in need of help.

By that time Jay and I would have made a deal with the devil himself to escape the heat of a blistering sun, so we agreed. When we got to Yuma, Jay and I had to pay fifteen cents a gallon for gasoline. That was high. Gasoline was only ten cents a gallon everywhere else. I had the feeling that fellow knew the price when he picked us up.

Ever since Jay and I had recovered from eating those canned sardines, we had not felt like eating very much and only snacked on junk food now and then. Being stuck out on that highway for most of the day in the hot sun and not having anything to eat all day, we were starving. We found a little cafe that advertised home cooking. Jay and I had T-bone steak, vegetables, potatoes, and everything that goes with a complete dinner, including coffee and it only cost us thirty-five cents each.

When Jay and I walked out of that cafe, I was so stuffed I was miserable. Jay mentioned he could hardly move and suggested we get hotel room for the night. I was considering his suggestion when I saw a train setting on a siding ready to move out. It was only about a half mile or more away.

Instead of staying on the street and walking around to the railroad yard. Jay and I thought we could save ourselves some steps and cut across country. To reach the railroad tracks we had to cross an area that had many adobe huts sitting here and there without any reason or beauty of design.

It seemed like every hut had three and four dogs to guard it. The dogs started to bark and growl and sounded as vicious as a pack of hungry wolves. Jay and I were not too worried since they were tied up and we were not doing anything wrong but walking across their property.

About that time several Indians came out of their adobe huts to investigate why the dogs were putting up such a fuss and they saw us. They began chasing us, yelling and waving sticks. Jay and I broke into a run. I cannot remember my feet ever touching the ground, I was running so fast. I was so scared that for the first time in my life I knew how the pony soldiers of days gone by felt when they found themselves surrounded by warlike Indians and had to run for their lives.

Just as Jay and I reached the train tracks, that freight train was pulling out, heading east, although at that time we would have jumped on any freight no matter what direction it was going. Jay and I escaped, but not without loss. I felt my hat slipping when I grabbed the ladder to jump on the train. I tried holding my head down to keep it from falling off; however, I had to make a choice. Let go of the ladder to save my hat or hang on and save my life. So that is how I lost my Stetson to the Indians. I really felt undressed being bare headed. Although I still had my scalp, I lost my fifty-dollar Stetson. Jay and I remained good friends the rest of our lives.

I thought I knew then what it was to be afraid. How little I knew. And with that I ended my tale of woe. For a little while I had kept my buddies entertained and our minds off our present miseries.

THEN ONE DAY THE GATES opened and fifteen to twenty big military trucks drove into the compound loaded with men and supplies. They were the American Embassy marines from Tensen and Peking. They were in full dress military uniforms with winter coats, gloves, fur hats, and warm boots. They had knit caps with face protectors that pulled down completely protecting the face from the cold. Those knit caps were made with holes for eyes, nose, and mouth. Not only that, those embassy marines were smoking American cigarettes. In fact they had a truckload of American cigarettes. We were most happy to see them and overjoyed just thinking about sharing their bounty.

There was also a crew of seaman with their captain. Theirs was an interesting story. They were on the ship that belonged to the president or the Wilson lines or something like that. They were to transport all the marines out of China to the Phillippines. Of course that was before the war started. The three hundred fifty embassy marines were the last ones to leave China and the ship was returning to get them.

The ship was about thirty miles from the mouth of the Yangtze river when the captain saw he was surrounded by Japanese war ships. The Japanese told him to leave or they were going to blow him out of the water. There was a little island close by, so he decided to scuttle the ship in the channel. He gave orders to open all the valves and for the men to abandoned ship. The captain headed the ship toward the channel and jumped into the water. But instead of the ship sinking, the darn thing ran aground on the island tearing an eighty-foot gash in the side of it.

The Japanese salvaged that ship, repaired that eighty-foot hole, and used that ship to haul American prisoners from the Phillippines to Japan. There was a big American bell on that ship and many American prisoners could not figure out what an American bell was doing on a Japanese ship–that was the reason.

I became friends with that captain. He was a good man. But to get back to my story about those embassy marines: The marines were surrounded by the Japanese and the Japanese told the marines that if they would surrender they could keep their store, their clothes, and all personal belongings, unlike how they treated the marines on Wake Island. So that was the reason they were so well dressed and had trucks full of food and supplies.

I would like to think the Japanese made that offer because of the casualties they suffered fighting a little more than three hundred marines on Wake Island and decided it was better to make a deal than to fight them in battle.

There were over two thousand men at Woo Sung when the embassy marines arrived and we were all cold, sick, and hungry. So naturally the first thing that came to our minds was how to convince them to share their warm clothes and canned food. Needless to say the order of the day was, "Let's make a deal and let the trading begin." Every man was for himself, except there was, one big problem. We did not have anything to trade and the most of us had to rely on the marines generosity and survived in the shadow of their kindnesses.

At first we were so ill-dressed that occasionally a marine just gave a coat or a pair of pants to someone. The marines had their names printed on all their clothes and when the marine saw his coat a week later on someone else other than the one he had given it to, that made him mad.

The marines did not understand just how bad off we were. They had not yet been exposed to hunger and cold and never realized how desperate we were. The coat that was given was traded for rice. We were that hungry.

Needless to say some men resorted to skullduggery while others resorted to just plain thievery. It was not long before the embassy marines thought everyone from Wake Island was nothing but a bunch of thieves.

A Martin and McCoy situation developed in the camp between us. Rather than let us have anything, the embassy marines shared their store with the men from Guam and the Hawaiians, and that made us mad. There was hard feelings for at least two months. Then the embassy marines started running low on food and wanted to trade cigarettes for extra food. They were not as good at trading as we were since that had been a way of life for us for a long time. It was not very long until they were down to the bare essentials and began to know the pain of hunger. That is when they became more understanding and all of us became friends again.

Outside the compound the land was covered with mounds. It was a Chinese graveyard. When the Chinese died they put the body in a wooden box and set the box on the ground and covered it up with dirt. They do not dig six-foot holes to bury their dead like we do. They keep stacking boxes on top of other boxes and covering them over with more dirt. Consequently some of those mounds get pretty big if it is a large family. As the bodies deteriorate the mounds get smaller in time.

When spring finally arrived the Japanese formed work parties to level that cemetery for gardens. Naturally when we started leveling burial sites, the Chinese raised a fuss for disturbing their dead.

The Japanese never had any compassion for the Chinese and seemed to enjoy killing them. They would shoot or bayonet them for no reason at all. Personalities of the two factions were at a fever pitch over that graveyard, and I thought for sure the Chinese were going to be killed. However, after negotiations the Chinese were given permission to remove their dead and what bones they could find and take them elsewhere.

It took several weeks to level that ground. Several trinkets of Jade were found and some men used those small baubles as collateral for more food. Treasures that no doubt had been buried with somebody's loved ones.

The Japanese gave us seeds and we planted them. Tread mills were built to bring water to the garden. We took loving care of that cultivated piece of ground. Never before had any garden had so many keepers. And just when we were ready to enjoy the fruits of our labors, the Japanese took a large share from our horn of plenty for themselves.

It was during that summer I worked digging a bigger canal through a swampy area that was invested with mosquitoes. I contracted malaria and maybe once in a great while I would be given quinine. Most of the men suffered from malaria or some other disease from the lack of medicine. There was everything from yellow jaundice to athlete's foot.

Under a guided tour of sorts the Red Cross was allowed to visit the camp. They took messages from a very few designated prisoners to send home to the U.S. The Red Cross even took requests for things from a certain few. One man asked for a guitar another man asked for a Bible. Everything was handled very properly under the watchful eyes of the Japanese guards.

We wanted to shout "more food, more medicine;" however, we were afraid to speak freely for fear of reprisal after the Red Cross left the scene. Nevertheless, I am sure they could see by our gaunt appearance, the dark circles under the eyes, and the lack of smiles that all was not as good as the Japanese wanted them to believe.

Later we were surprised when a guitar and several Bibles arrived. The Red Cross sent hundreds of care packages, one package per man, and the Japanese stored them in a warehouse. Unfortunately the Red Cross trusted the Japanese to distribute the care boxes. Consequently, we were lucky if we received anything.

After the Japanese helped themselves we received half a box. One man complained about that and asked the guard how the Japanese determined exactly what a half of box consisted of. The guard unsheathed his sword and brought that sword down across that care package as hard as he could splitting it in two.

"That's how," the guard said angrily. "Any other questions?" the guard added, holding his sword ready to strike. Needless to say, silence prevailed.

You could live on what food the Japanese gave you providing you never got sick or you never had to work to use up any energy. The men were constantly trading whatever they had to get a little more food. That summer and fall, days passed in slow succession doing monotonous labor without reward. None of us were looking forward to another winter and all too soon it was upon us. We faced that winter in pretty bad shape. We were in fairly good shape the last winter and we barely survived that one. I worried about my friends. I was not a big man so I could survive on what little food the Japanese gave us, but some of the larger men could not.

Whenever I lost a friend to the dark angel of death, I would fall into a state of depression, and to keep my sanity and soul together I would mentally transport myself to the past again. I survived the cold when I was younger and I would somehow survive the cold in China.

Chapter Eleven

WE WERE AT THAT SO-CALLED MODEL CAMP FOR TEN MONTHS before being transferred to Kiang Wang POW camp, which was only five or six miles away. The men who had been gathering parts to build a radio cleverly managed to take all the parts with them with the help of several others. Everyone carried a little piece, a screw here a little piece of wire there. Everything looked very innocent.

The barracks we were put in were built with an enclosed room at one end that was originally used for an office. That room was still being used as an office of sorts. The man in charge of our barracks stayed in there. When the radio was finally finished, he hid it behind a section of the wall in his room. So far all we could do was receive news; we could not send. When he felt it was safe, he would bring that radio out and we would try to find a station we could understand. We longed for news about the war.

There was not a man in camp who did not know about that radio. I do not know all the circumstances that made one of the prisoners inform on us. I do not know if he did it to save his life or trade information for more food or just what happened, but an American prisoner told the Japanese about that radio.

The grapevine we had was faster than any telegraph. Word was sent to the barracks the Japanese were on their way to search the place. The radio was quickly disposed of. One of the men threw it into the outside latrine.

A large open trench had been dug with toilet seats installed over it. It was nothing but a long, giant outhouse. The Chinese cleaned that trench out periodically and used the contents on their vegetable gardens.

When the Japanese guards arrived we played very dumb. Hear no evil, see no evil, and speak no evil. Of course they did not believe us and tore that place apart. The guards really became upset and abusive when they never found anything. I was genuinely scared that we all would be in a box by sundown.

I do not know how the Japanese discovered the radio had been thrown in that trench, but they did and made us dig in that slimy, stinky mess until the radio was found I was relieved that we were not shot. I guess the Japanese thought that digging through all that crap was punishment enough. Needless to say we never built anymore radios.

We could see the skyline of Shanghai from Kiang Wang. I knew that ships from all over the world docked at Shanghai. At night I would think about sailing home. I would make believe I was standing at the bow of a big ship on my way to Hawaii. My thoughts were so real I could feel the sea breeze brush across my face and smell the fragrances of the tropical flowers of the islands. But when I reached Hawaii I could not leave the ship. I could only gaze wistfully across the Pacific yearning to be home. I could not even get to San Francisco anymore, not even in my dreams.

My speculations that things could get worse became a reality. Living conditions were brutal. Winter had set in and we did not have any heat. Kiang Wang was the pit of hell. There were no good days in that camp. Only long days of misery, hard labor, starvation and death. Death became an inviting pathway to escape the cruelty that existed there.

We had not been there a week until a guard shot Loney Riddle through the neck and killed him. Loney was on the inside of that electric fence and the guard was on the outside. Although the guard told his commander it was an accident, I will always believe he shot Loney on purpose. I think Loney was the first prisoner to be shot at Kiang Wang.

Everyday a Japanese guard called out about a hundred numbers and those men were taken and used for slave labor up to sixteen and eighteen hours a day. There were times when the men never returned and we never saw them again. The Japanese did everything they could to discourage us. But the more they tried, the more I resolved to survive no matter what. We were fed about a cup of rice twice a day. The bedbugs ate better than we did; they chewed on us night and day. Some of the men were so sick and weak from the lack of food the electric fence that surrounded Kiang Wang became the final solution to end their misery. Never before were the words made more plain to me, "There are times when it is more difficult to live than to die."

Imagine my surprise when my number was called and I was taken to the back of the barracks and a Japanese guard asked my name. There was a microphone there and I did not know what to think. Then I saw a recording machine and thought I was going to make a talking letter. I was chosen quite by random to be questioned for propaganda. I was disappointed when I learned that I could not speak freely and all questions were carefully prepared. What I did not know until after the war was that a ham radio operator in Washington happened to pick up that broadcast and got in touch with my folks to let them know I was all right.

After the broadcast I was allowed to rest. I could not help but wonder if the Japanese was going to send that recording to America, to my folks, and I fell into the dimension of my dreamworld.

I DECIDED TO HITCHHIKE AND hop trains to New Blaine, Arkansas to see Dad. I was walking at a good pace along the highway when a familiar pick-up whizzed by me and came to a screeching halt. I heard a familiar voice call my name. It was June Tulk. He asked me where I was going, and when I told him Arkansas he insisted on buying a roundtrip bus ticket for me and gave me fifty dollars spending money. He told me I could work it out when I returned.

I had to admit it was much better riding the bus and not having to worry about where your next ride was coming from or what freight you had to catch or where to hide from the bulls to keep them from taking you to jail. *Bulls* was the name the hobos gave the men who patrolled the freight trains. Their job was to keep the hobos from getting a free ride. Some of those bulls were pretty mean and downright hateful.

At first the bus seats were soft and comfortable, but after hours of sitting, those same seats became hard and uncomfortable. It seemed like the farther east we traveled, the worse the weather became. It started raining and I could not see anything out the window at night except my own reflection. I snuggled down in my seat and tried to sleep. I thought that bus was never going to get to Arkansas.

Finally, after thirty-six hours of traveling, the bus driver called out, "Everyone for New Blaine, this is it." He called out just like several people were getting off, except I was the only one. It was about midnight and rain-ing. I grabbed my suitcase and stepped off the bus. I was on a hill, in front of a service station that was closed. I turned and asked the driver where the town was.

"It is out there across the canyon," the driver replied.

"And this is where you are going to leave me? On top of this hill in the rain where there is nothing! It is the middle of the night, for God's sake."

"I am sorry but this is the bus stop for New Blaine," the driver said.

I could sense the bus driver felt badly about my situation and wanted to help so he added, "See that light down there about a hundred yards from the bottom of the hill? Well walk down there toward that light. It is the first house after you pass the school house. Those folks are pretty friendly and will probably let you spend the night."

With that bit of advice he closed the bus door and slowly drove away. There I stood with only the doleful sound of raindrops hitting the metal roof of the service station to break the silence of the night. Rather than stay there until daylight, I decided to take the bus driver's advice and I started walk-ing toward the light.

I wondered about the wisdom of waking up strangers in the middle of the night to ask them if they had a place for me to sleep until morning. I silently whispered, "God help me."

When I reached the bottom of the hill I heard live hillbilly music being played and the sound was coming from the house with the porch light. The music playing was happy and very inviting. At least I would not be waking up anyone from a sound sleep. That thought alone eased my anxiety and prompted me to hurry.

I walked up the steps and stood on the porch just to listen. When the music stopped I knocked on the front door. A young man answered and before I could say anything he said, "Come on in, Skeet."

I could not believe my ears. He knew my younger brother and thought I was he. I stepped inside and there were three other young men holding musical instruments. One held a mandolin, another a guitar, and the other a violin. The young man who let me in turned to look at me and said, "You are not Skeet."

I explained who I was, and they not only welcomed me but drove me to Dad's place at Happy Hollow. I told them thank you and I grabbed my things. As soon as I stepped out of the car they drove off before I could ask them to wait. I did not want them to leave until I was sure somebody was there. It was dark and I could just barely make out the outline of a great big house on top of the hill.

It must have been three o'clock in the morning when I nervously knocked on the front door hoping to see a familiar face. Dad opened the door and with great happiness grabbed me and threw his arms around me to give a big hug. One by one the family came to investigate what all the hell-a-boo was about, and they were as happy to see me as I was them. Since everyone was already out of bed, we had breakfast and visited until dawn.

I found Arkansas a very peaceful place. The people were easy going. Speed was not everything and they were not in a hurry to do anything, not even their plowing. They never seemed to get excited about anything.

The people were self-sufficient, too. They made everything from roof shingles to soap and hominy. They raised their own tobacco and it seemed like all the men chewed tobacco. I never met anyone there that did not like music. Music was their main entertainment. I listened to some of the best mountain music I had ever heard while staying in Arkansas. Happy Hollow was a ways from town so a grocery truck came once a week and stopped at every house. The grocery driver took orders and delivered everything the following week. For those who did not have any money, the grocery driver traded for eggs, milk, cream, butter, fresh vegetables, chickens, or whatever they had to trade.

Even though I had only seen pictures I embellished the truth and told Dad of the magnificent scenic wonders in California: the big trees, crystal blue lakes, and rivers running everywhere. I told Dad they had more fruit raised in that state than any other I had been to. At least I had seen the fruit orchards. Dad got excited and thought he would like to move to California. He had not found the prosperous opportunities in Arkansas that he was led to believe existed there.

I stayed with Dad that winter and I returned to Roswell when lambing started. June needed me and was overjoyed to see me. I was one of the best sheep cutters around. Of course I must give my horse, Cherry, a little credit for that honor. I really felt like I had come home working for June. Cherry was well-rounded and needed exercise. June had taken good care of him. It felt good having Cherry to ride every day. I was very happy.

Two weeks after I had arrived a killer storm hit the plains with freezing temperatures that fell way below zero. The storm stalled over the area and lasted longer than expected. The weather was so cold the fog froze on the net wire and it made the fences look like they were made of brick. The ice kept building up until the pastures were covered with snow and ice that was as hard as a rock. June lost thirty percent of the lambs.

Finally the cold spell was broken. The sun came out in full splendor and warmed the land. The ice melted and lots of little yellow flowers bloomed. The lambs ate the flowers and died–the flowers were poison. June lost another thirty percent of his lambs. That spring was disastrous for June.

It was well into summer when I was riding to the ranch at days' end and I could see the distorted image of what looked like a car. Since it was flat country without any trees whatsoever, you could see mirages of things three miles away. The mirages might look real long or real tall, but I had seen enough mirages to enable me to make out what they were.

When I reached the ranch, Dad, Skeet, and Syble were there. Dad came to tell me he had gone into a partnership with my cousin, Roy King, on a ranch in Paskenta, California. Dad opened a California road map to show me its location. Paskenta was just a tiny dot on the map. Today Paskenta is a dying community.

Roy King always wanted to be a cowboy. However, he was a much better insurance salesman than he was a cowboy, so Roy offered Dad a full partnership if he would come to California and work the ranch. Roy needed Dad as much as Dad needed Roy, and that partnership proved to be the betterment for both of them.

Dad had left Iva and the children in Texas with Iva's mother until he could afford to bring them to Paskenta. Skeet did not want to stay with Iva, so Dad brought Skeet to stay with me. Syble came along for the ride. Dad was going to ride the bus to California. Roy and Dad bought four hundred head of cattle to stock the ranch, and Red was already at the ranch in Paskenta taking care of the cattle until Dad could get there. Before Dad left for California, he wanted to be sure I would bring Iva and the children to Paskenta when he sent for us. I already knew that nothing was going to stop me from going to California, so I agreed.

The days passed slowly until a month had gone by. Skeet and I received a letter from Dad wanting us to bring the family to Paskenta. I told June it was time for me to leave, and I walked to the corral to tell Cherry goodbye but I could not. I had the most foreboding feeling I would never see Cherry again, so I decided I had to buy him back even if I had to ride him every step of the way to California. I was not going to leave my horse again. I turned to go to the house and June was standing behind me. I did not hear him walk up.

"June, I would like to buy back Cherry."

"The way you are bumming around it is not good for a horse. Cherry has a good home here and no one rides him but me when you are not here."

I could see that June loved Cherry and did not want to lose him. I knew in my heart Cherry had a wonderful home there and I also knew that June was right. Until I settled down I did not need a horse. June had always been so good to me over the years and he had already lost so much that year, I could not bring myself to take Cherry away from him, too. I changed my mind. It was all I could do to keep the tears back when I patted Cherry for the last time and told him goodbye.

As I walked away I turned and took one last look at Cherry and everything familiar to me and said a silent goodbye. I wondered if I ever would come back again. My emotions surfaced and I became melancholy. I could feel the tears forming in my eyes and I was having a hard time holding them back. A loud scream brought me once again to reality.

THE ELECTRIC FENCE THAT SURROUNDED Kiang Wang was built very low to the ground and about six feet high. There were a lot of rats at that camp. It was a common sight to see the charred remains of a rat laying at the bottom of that fence. When a rat ran under the electric fence, the rat was burned to a crisp if his tail barely touched it.

If the grass was allowed to grow and touch the electric fence, it shorted it out. To keep that from happening, every so often the Japanese had the old men cut the grass under the electric fence with a little hand *sei*.

Dutch Raspy was the boss of the Americans who trimmed the grass. It was his job to tell the Japanese to turn off the electricity before the old men started to trim. On one occasion one of the men shouted to Dutch that the fence was still on after Dutch had told the Japanese to turn it off. Dutch foolishly grabbed it with his hand to show the fence was not live and it almost killed him. It was his scream that brought me to attention.

Fortunately Dutch had many big-headed tacks on the bottom of his shoes to keep them from wearing out. I do not know that much about electricity, but those tacks allowed the electricity to go through him without killing him. However, the force broke both his feet and ruined his heart, but he survived to talk about it. Personally I thought the Japanese purposely left the electricity on. They were that mean.

The only other person to survive electrocution after hitting that fence was a young Chinese man who we called Philadelphia because that is where he was from. He accidently fell and was froze to it. The jolt knocked him out. We worked on him for hours trying to revive him. Hot water was poured over him and several men took turns rubbing him and rubbing him. Then more hot water was poured over him and the rubbing continued. After hours of treatment he came to. Unfortunately, the inside of his hands had the skin completely burned off and his fingers on one hand curled into his hand and grew to the palms. Dutch and Philadelphia are the only two I know of who ever survived after touching that fence.

Despite all the meanness there was a Japanese doctor who tried in his own way to help relieve the suffering, and that was not easy when he was also under the uncaring eyes of his superiors. The doctor could not show us very much mercy or his own life would have been in jeopardy. Not only that, he was given very little medicine to use for our benefit.

When new prisoners arrived I always wanted to know how things were on the outside. The news was never good. When we heard the Japanese had taken the Philippine Islands and were marching across China like a grass fire. I could not understand how such a thing could happen. I would not accept the belief that the Japanese were going to win the war. I just could not imagine Hirohito in the White House and I refused to give up hope.

There was a large piece of ground north of the camp that looked like it had a bunch of sand hills on it. Of course I knew it was another Chinese cemetery. We were ordered to level that forty acres and plant another garden. The Chinese raised a fuss again and were finally allowed to remove their dead. The Chinese gathered the dead and bones as fast as the men dug them up.

It took us six months to make another garden spot of that area, too. When I worked I would always remember the times when I was bumming around and lived on fresh vegetables I had taken from fields along the road. I always wanted to be a rancher but never a farmer, and here I was planting another garden for the enemy.

It was about that time Mel Davidson's number was called and he had to work on a detail clearing a warehouse of food supplies. As he was working, he noticed a big sack sitting in the corner that had broken open. Mel was certain the sack contained food of some sort. Every time he passed that sack and the guards were not looking he would grab a big handful of whatever the sack contained and stuff it into his pockets. By the time he returned to the barracks his pockets were bulging. I was surprised the guards never noticed. Or maybe they did and wanted a good laugh.

Mel anxiously took out a handful to see what he had. He held a handful of dried grasshoppers. I broke out laughing. One of the men told us that was a very good source of protein so Mel closed his eyes and ate one. He told us it was not that bad and shared his plunder. So we all tried eating a grasshopper or two since we were so hungry.

It was inevitable that I would become deathly sick from dysentery, and death hung in my shadow. Everyone had dysentery and most everyone had walking pneumonia, too. I barely weighed a hundred pounds. In my delirium I remembered the desperate years of the Great Depression when I was a teenager and could not find work. I was hungry and cold a lot of time then and had no place to stay, yet I knew the freedom of body and spirit. I thought of those years as the good old days as I lay on my death bed.

In spite of my determination to live, my health kept deteriorating until I no longer cared whether I lived or not. I was ready to face the Grim Reaper, to give up the fight and surrender to the Dark Angel of Death. Mentally I would sink back into the past and relive those days when I was most happy.

A good friend of mine named Gancy, who worked in the kitchen, came to see me. Gancy was worried that I might not make it. I was so ill I barely remember him talking to me. Gancy had worked with me on Wake Island and had been placed as kitchen help in China. He saved my life when he requested my help. I was made to get up and go to work making tea and washing dishes.

At least it was warm in the kitchen, and when I washed the pans I nonchalantly rubbed my finger around the inside edge and scraped the scum from the cooked rice and ate it. Of course if I had been caught doing that, I would have been shot. We were threatened with instant death if we took so much as one grain of rice. Yet I considered myself lucky to be there and ever so slowly I began to recover.

Every time I made tea I wished I had some loco weed to put in it. I remembered how horses would go crazy after eating it. How I wished I could get my hands on some of that weed to mix with the tea leaves. I would get a smile on my face just thinking about the Japanese guards lying on their backs with their eyes crossed and their legs in the air. The cook always wanted to know what I had to smile about.

"Nothing," I would answer. It was better to keep your thoughts to yourself.

Although I survived, I lived with guilt because I worked in the kitchen where it was warm, while my comrades were freezing and starving to death in those barracks. Because of being accused by some of the men who thought I was eating some of their share, I never permitted myself to take one grain of rice extra than I was allowed.

The men never realized what pressure we were under in the kitchen. Cooking and smelling the food and knowing we dare not even taste it. There was a Japanese sergeant in charge of food distribution, and he had Japanese guards watching our every move. It was immediate death if they even thought you were taking more food than you were allowed.

Every day, guards came in to get men. Sometime only two or three and sometime twenty-five or thirty. Nobody knew where they went and we would never see them again. There was not a man there who did not long to escape, but we were in a land peopled by a race who looked strange to us and we could not understand their language. We did not have a chance in hell.

Meantime the Japanese commander of the camp came up with the idea of building his own personal mountain retreat, except there were no mountains there. Even though I worked in the kitchen, I was not excused from working on other projects.

The men, including me, were outfitted with yo-ho poles. That was the Chinese idea of a carryall. A yo-ho pole was a long pole with a basket at each end, and you carried it across your shoulder. The poles were also used to move the Chinese sampans through the many canals around Shanghai. We were worked as hard as any slaves in the dark ages.

At first we thought we were building a rifle range. When we started, the base was probably four hundred yards long and four hundred feet wide. We carried yo-ho poles with baskets of dirt for a quarter-mile before dumping them. Men were kept at the base to level the dirt as we poured it out. We kept piling dirt higher and higher. When it became obvious it was not a rifle range, I could not imagine what we were making or what the end result could possibly be. We were working eighteen hours a day, and evidently the work was not going fast enough to suit the Japanese commander because he had us lay rails for little mining carts that were given to us. Those carts were not like our American mining carts. They were made of wood. It was just a little flat car with a wooden box on top that we had to dump by hand.

As the pile of dirt took on the shape of a large mound, then a giant hill to become a small mountain. We named that self made mountain, "Mount Fujiyama." We kept piling dirt and the mountain kept growing higher. When the mountain was built up to a certain point we had to tear the tracks up and build a new ramp to relay the rails. I wondered if we could be building another tower of Babel.

The higher the mountain the more men it took to push those little mining carts up the hill. By the time the men reached the top they were exhausted, and after dumping the carts the men rode them down. Without any weight in those carts they built up so much speed that they sometimes would jump the tracks. As the mountain kept getting higher and higher, those tracks were so steep that it became very dangerous riding down in them. Men had been killed and many more injured when the carts jumped the tracks and rolled on them as the carts rolled over and over down the mountain. Those accidents were becoming more and more frequent. I never wanted that happening to me, so I gouged a hole in the bottom of the mining cart and used a stick to hold against the back wheels to slow it down. It took at least two, sometimes three, men to hold that stick tightly enough to slow those wheels. That worked so well everyone tried it.

Then came the day I was not paying attention and the cart that several of us were riding in jumped the track and over we went. Fortunately no one in the cart was killed; they only suffered from cuts and bruises. I was not so lucky. Although the cart missed rolling on me and I survived the fall, I injured my back quite badly. I would suffer the rest of my life with back trouble.

It was my understanding that Mount Fujiyama was to be built up to four hundred feet high and wide enough at the top to lay a highway, for whatever reason I never knew, and I still do not know to this day. It was about two hundred feet high when I was transferred to another camp in the latter part of 1943. I have often wondered if that mountain was ever completed. I was moved with over six hundred other prisoners to Osaka, Japan, to work in the shipyards there. Again I had to leave many friends whom I would never see again.

Chapter Twelve

I SAW JOHNNY MCCLOUD A COUPLE OF TIMES in the prison camp in China, but when I left China I never saw him again. I do not know whatever happened to him. I have often wondered if he made it through the war.

We were marched to Shanghai and put aboard a freighter. I was not way down in the hold that time, and we were treated much better than we were on the *Nitta Maru*. In the afternoon the captain allowed several men at a time to be brought up on deck for ten minutes. Those who had any cigarettes could smoke at that time. It took about four days to sail to Osaka.

All the men prayed the next POW camp would not be so harsh. Most men thought things could not get any worse. Nevertheless, every time we moved things became worse and I began to think there was not a God. When we landed at Osaka, the sun had just disappeared over the horizon and the evening shadows were quickly enveloping us. Yet there was still enough daylight to see plainly, and I was not impressed with the area.

The Japanese hurried us off the ship and lined us up on the dock in a military formation. Ivan Carden was standing next to me. The Japanese guard in charge stood at the front and center of the formation and pointed right down a line of men that was between Ivan and me. Ivan had to step to the right and I had to step to the left. Ivan was sent to another camp and I went to a camp located in Osaka that was very close to the shipyards. I knew I was going to miss Ivan. He had been my buddy for a year and half and we were as close as brothers. I never saw Ivan again until after the war. He lives with his wife Ada in Lodi, California. We have remained friends all our lives.

The camp was next to a river and many English and Australian prisoners were there already. There were three separate shipyards in the immediate area. Whatever shipyard you were sent to, that was where you stayed until you died from disease or starved, froze, beaten, or just plain worked to death.

We were rousted out before dawn, given a bowl of rice, and herded down to the river, where we boarded a large motor launch. It was something like the lifeboats you see on today's cruise ships, except the Japanese motor launch had a sound all its own. With a full load of men the motor labored *chug-a-chug, chug-a-chug,* as the boat moved slowly across the river.

The river emptied into a large bay. On the north side of the bay was Kobe and on the south side was Osaka. I was taken to the shipyard that I thought was built on an island, but it could have been at the end of a peninsula. I was never quite sure.

I was put to drilling holes on a huge sheet of brass about thirty feet long that was destined to be riveted to the side of a ship. I was never mechanically inclined so I never knew what I was doing most of the time. I was never quite sure if I was doing it right and merely went through the motions.

Next I was put on an enormous piece of rough brass about thirty feet long that had to be put on a mammoth lathe, to smooth it out to make a drive shaft. Then I was put to work running a drill press—a great big rascal. I had to drill holes about the size of a match stick through flat plates to make peak traps.

I had to sign for every drill bit I needed, and if I broke a bit regardless of the reason, the Japanese thought it was sabotage and I would be beaten—although there was plenty of sabotage going on right under their noses, everything from bad rivets to poor construction. Anything we thought we could getaway with and would cause them unrelenting grief later on.

The Japanese boss in charge of our building was called a three-striped hauncho. There were one-stripe haunchos and two-stripe haunchos. By the time a man was promoted to a three-stripe hauncho, he was older and had a certain amount of clout.

The hauncho in charge of our building was a real nice older Japanese man. Whenever we broke a bit he would turn in the broken bit for a new one and tell his superiors that he had already punished us. He saved us from having several beatings. He had a gentle soul and I liked him.

There was a young man working behind me named Tommy Sanford. He was from Oregon. Tommy had a bunch of stuff bolted to his table in his effort to hold whatever he was working on. He was using a one-and-half-inch bit. The weather was pretty cold and the building was not heated, so Tommy wore a pair of mittens. Every once in awhile he'd reach around and brush off the metal shavings from around the bit.

One cold day the inevitable happened when Tommy did not turn off the drill press before wiping the metal shavings away. The bit caught his mitten and twisted his arm around then caught his shirt sleeve. Tommy screamed for help. I looked around and it had his arm twisted clear to the shoulder. At first I thought the drill had come loose and fallen on him. There was blood everywhere. I rushed to cut off the electricity. That is when I saw his arm all twisted around. It was awful. There were two separate bones sticking out of the flesh at least two inches.

I tied off what I could to keep Tommy from bleeding to death. Four of us put him on a litter made out of straw sacks and carried him three miles to a hospital through three feet of snow. For the first time I was thankful for the bitter cold. That alone probably kept Tommy from bleeding to death.

When we finally reached the hospital, Tommy was not given any pain killers or anything. The four of us lifted him on the table and we had to hold him down for three hours while a Japanese doctor cut his arm open to straighten out the bones, drill holes in them and tie steel wire through the holes to hold the bones in place. Then the doctor sewed Tommy's arm up and put a cast around that arm and his chest all the way down to his waist.

When the doctor finished we carried Tommy back to the barracks. With nothing but a cast around him to keep him warm, Tommy shivered so hard I heard his teeth clicking together. He thought he was going to freeze to death before we made it back to the barracks. At least the cold kept his mind off his pain.

Tommy survived the prison camps and returned home. I would like to tell everyone that Tommy lived happily ever after. Unfortunately I cannot. He died a hopeless alcoholic, but it seems to every sad story there is something good that arises from it. After the war Mel Davidson and I met Tommy's sister Marjorie. Mel fell in love and married her. They are still happily married today and living in Grants Pass, Oregon. When Marjorie wanted to know about her brother, I told her how Tommy was hurt and the pain he suffered. We have remained good friends through the years.

There was another friend of mine who became ill from a bad tooth. He became so sick he was taken to the hospital. My friend was also a spiritual leader of sorts. He was not an ordained minister or a priest or anything like that, just a good man who tried to help keep our spiritual needs alive by holding services once in awhile on Sunday.

While in the hospital my friend developed pneumonia. Without any medicine he became deathly sick and the doctor had to drain his lungs every other day. My friend's temperature shot up to one hundred six degrees and the doctor held little hope.

That very night my friend had a dream or a vision; he was not sure. A figure with long hair, dressed in a white robe and wearing sandals stood at the foot of his bed. The figure told my friend that he had a lot of work to do so he was going to recover. The figure told him to get up and walk with him. They walked all around the hospital before my friend returned to his bed. The next morning my friend did not have a temperature and his lungs were clear of fluid. The doctor was dumbfounded. A miracle had transpired that the doctor could not explain. After four days my friend returned to work. After listening to what had happened to my friend, I had second thoughts about whether there was a God. My friend wrote his own experiences after the war and I felt privileged when he sent me a copy of his manuscript.

We were given a gallon can of charcoal every two weeks with which to heat the barracks. That seemed to be the amount allowed for all prison camps, at least the ones I was in. That worked out to be about two briquets a day. Those briquets were about the size of a small biscuit. Not very much to be thankful for, but at least we were out of the weather.

We had two days off every month, usually on a Sunday. Sometime we had to clean the toilets on one of those days off. The other we would take a bath and steam our clothes to get the lice out of them. That was not always easy to accomplish since there were so many prisoners and only one place to bathe and one big wash pot.

The days passed in long repetitious, mundane labor. It seemed no matter how hard we worked we just could not please the Japanese and there were more beatings. The longer we were there the more brutal the beatings were becoming. When the Japanese wanted to punish everyone in camp, they would cut our food rations without any explanation, and we were already living on next to nothing. Of course we never had any way of knowing that the war was not going well for them, and I believe they took their frustrations out on us.

Despite all the chaos and brutality shown to us by the military, I must tell about a few civilians who were not like that. Like all races there are good and bad, and there were a few kind hearts who gave us salt now and then. Of course that was done without the Japanese guards knowing about it.

The Japanese became savagely mean. They made us stand at attention while they beat us across the back with a stick of bamboo about four feet long with one end taped with black tape for a good hand-hold, whereas the other end was split up several inches. Every time you were struck it was like being hit with a whip called "cat of nine tails." It made little difference whether it was made from leather or bamboo, the results were the same: With every blow you suffered bleeding cuts.

The other bamboo sticks used were made with several holes drilled through them. When you were struck with those, it took the skin off. Because of our poor condition, wherever those holes hit, sores would develop and infection would set in. Before those sores could heal, we would be beaten again for absolutely nothing.

The Grim Reaper was no stranger but an invited guest. Death was our only hope of escape. And yet I could not bring myself to surrender my life. I still held fast to the belief the Japanese were going to be very sorry someday, and I wanted to be around to see it. My body and mind were deteriorating; I could not hold a thought for very long. I used to always dream of sailing home and I could not even reach the boat anymore. It was as if my whole system was shutting down, and I would have to resort to my past so

I could mentally visit home and family again. My thoughts returned to the time I brought Iva and the children to Paskenta.

I NEVER THOUGHT I WOULD ever want to see Peacock, Texas; yet, I was so anxious to get there I could hardly stand it. When I reached Iva's mother's house, I was happily surprised to find Coley there, too. I assumed he was not able to patch things up with Rosie since he was there alone. Iva had things packed and ready to go since they knew I was on my way. After a big farewell dinner, it did not take very long for Coley, Skeet, and me to pack the car.

You would not believe how much stuff we managed to cram into that Model B. We would have made the *Grapes of Wrath* look like a luxury trip. We had three mattresses tied on top. We built rods on the back that stuck way out so we could carry an extra large box three feet high, three feet wide, and four feet long. I do not know what was inside—I only knew it was heavy.

You could not see the back seat or the floorboards. Quilts were folded and stacked level to the backs of the front seats. More belongings and suitcases were crammed into the fender wells. Pots and pans were hanging at every available spot and clanked together at every bump in the road. If you could not see us coming, there is not a doubt in my mind that you could have heard us. Boxes were stacked and tied to the running boards and we could not open the rear doors. Like chickens in a coop Syble, Billike, Nina Mae, and Frank rode in back atop the quilts. Iva and my new baby half-sister Thelma, Coley, Skeet, and I rode in the front seat.

That old Model B was already so worn out I worried that we might not make it to the county line. Every time we filled up with gas, we had to fill up with oil, too. So we would ask the station attendant if he had any used oil we could buy, and that is what we used—nothing but old used oil. That old Model B looked liked it was on fire going down the highway.

We were not ten miles out of Peacock when baby Thelma started crying and became car sick and would remain sick for the whole trip. It seemed we were always short on money and long on determination. Skeet, Coley, and I took turns driving. We had planned on driving night and day until we reached the ranch at Paskenta. In those days you had to buy water. All along the highway were signs for free air and water with every fill-up. We never got thirsty because we needed gas about every time we needed a drink of water.

It was a hundred degrees when we passed through Arizona. The baby was still sick and Iva and the girls were very tired. We stopped to rest at a hotel in Kingman, Arizona, that charged one dollar fifty cents a day. We rented one room. We did not have the money to get everyone their own rooms. The room was about fourteen by fourteen and no cooler. But at least Iva and the baby had a bed to sleep in. The rest of us lay around on the floor.

The railroad tracks ran alongside the hotel, and every time a fast-moving freight train rolled by, whether it was during the day or in the middle of the night, it shook that hotel room as if in an earthquake. The train would awaken the baby and then none of us were able to get very much rest, let alone any sound sleep. We stayed in that hotel room for three days. The temperature cooled at night to an uncomfortable ninety degrees. That was still a relief from the three-digit heat we had to endure every day. I was told that the inspection station at the California border would never let us through with those old mattresses on the account of bugs. I took affront at that; because never having any money did not mean we were filthy.

When I told the family we might lose the mattresses at the inspection station, Iva worried. We talked it over and decided to keep them and chance it. We needed everything we had. That was not the only problem we had to worry about. Iva did not have a pink slip on the car. Skeet traded for it in Arkansas, and all Iva had was a bill of sale written on a piece of tablet paper describing the car.

We finally left Kingman and I worried every mile of the way whether we would be allowed into California with all our things. I thought about cutting across country to miss the station, but we were lucky to be making it down the highway let alone trying to cross any hills without a road.

We pulled into the inspection station at Barstow, California, and I crossed my fingers. I thought it might help the situation and improve the chances of keeping everything.

A man in uniform walked slowly toward us. He skeptically eyed every inch of the car. When he reached the driver's side he leaned over and looked inside. Without a word he stood up straight and walked sort of stiff-legged completely around the car. I just knew we had had it and expected him to tell us to get out and unload everything. I really thought that was going to be the end of the trip right then and there.

He leaned over once more and with authority asked to see the papers on the car. I handed him the only papers we had. He read them carefully and told me to wait. He walked into the station and came out carrying a wire brush. He lifted the hood and scrubbed off the numbers on the motor. He wrote them down and told us we could go. I could not believe what I was hearing. We had not been there ten minutes. The more we talked about that situation the more I thought he let us go through because he was afraid we might break down and he would not know what to do with us.

Once through that inspection station, our souls were lifted and we felt on top of the world. That was the last big hurdle and there was nothing to stop us then. We all were riding on a crest of exuberant happiness.

We drove constantly until we reached an orange stand shaped like a giant orange just out of Orland, California. There was a big sign, ALL THE ORANGE JUICE YOU CAN DRINK FOR TEN CENTS. All of us were so thirsty we drank and drank and drank. It is a wonder we did not put them out of business. Once we were filled with orange juice, we returned to Highway 99.

We were all getting excited by then. Orland was only ten miles from Corning and Paskenta was only twenty miles from Corning. When we turned off Highway 99 to go toward Paskenta our excitement was building to such a pitch that we could hardly stand it. My eyes started searching for any sign of Paskenta. Oak trees grew in abundance on the low-lying foothills. The land looked like good cattle country.

When I reached Paskenta, I stopped at what looked like a general store. It was a combination bar and grocery store that sold everything from sewing needs to plumbing supplies. The man behind the counter knew the ranch and exactly how to get there. He drew me a little map.

The ranch was located toward Log Springs and I saw a large mountain in that direction. I knew that old car would never make it over that steep of a climb. I cannot tell you the relief I felt when I came to three large pine poles across the road that served as a gate of sorts with Dad's brand across it. I did not have to drive over that mountain that stood like a pillar in the distance. I had worried for nothing. I drove through the gate and I followed two wheel tracks for half a mile before we finally reached the house.

What a joyous feeling when I pulled up in the front yard and I knew we had at last reached our destination. We had made it. The trip was over. It had ended on a happy note without any more problems, and for that I was thankful. I just wanted to shout a big hooray. A real old-fashioned family reunion followed.

With those recollections I almost broke out crying. I finally had to stop myself from thinking about anything except getting some sleep while I had the chance. I was tired of thinking about the past and I promised myself that somehow I would survive to see my home again.

THE RIGOR-OF SLAVE LABOR was draining every drop of stamina I possessed and was definitely taking a toll. There were at the least four or five deaths every night in that prison camp. When a man died he was unceremoniously taken outside the camp and cremated. The whole process was done with all the compassion given to a nuisance value. I was told the ashes were put in a box with the man's name or number on it and stored somewhere in a warehouse to be sent to the United States when the war ended. I do not know if that was ever fulfilled.

When prisoners were brought into camp from other prison camps to replace the dead, more stories of brutality and torture were revealed. For a country that was supposed to be a civilized nation, Japan was barbarous and cruel. They still believed in mass punishment and torturing their prisoners.

Finally came the day the air-raid sirens went off. We were herded outside and I looked up and saw about thirty streaks way up across the sky. The streaks were all in a formation. None of us knew what those streaks were since we had never seen them before. At that time we had never heard of vapor trails. The Japanese never told us those were American planes overhead. The planes passed over us and flew to bomb somewhere else that time.

In the days to come there were many more raids, and it did not take us very long to figure out what was happening. One night the sirens went off about quarter to eleven. The bombing started and bombs fell constantly until four in the morning. The planes kept flying over like an endless chain belt. They just kept coming. Not one bomb came inside the compound where we were located. We thought for sure those pilots knew where we were. We felt as safe as if we were in church as long as we stayed inside the barracks.

The next morning I heard that sixty percent of Kobe and Osaka had been destroyed. At last my dreams were coming true. The Japanese people were starting to feel the sting of war in their own backyard. My hopes were renewed and my faith restored. I was filled with a new determination to survive.

During that long bombing raid was the first time we had ever seen fire-bombs. Sometimes those fire-bombs exploded way up in the air and spread fires over a large area. When they blew up, a rubberlike substance was spread everywhere—little pieces that smelled like gasoline, yet burned like rubber and stuck like glue to anything they landed on. No matter what the Japanese tried, they could not put the fire out. There were fires burning everywhere in every direction. Only sand could smother the fires and bring them under control, and sand was not readily available. At that time we had never heard of napalm, so we called them fire-bombs. The fires continued burning until there was not anything left that would burn.

The bombs hit right up to the road that led into our compound but never fell inside where we were. That is when I was positive the pilots knew where we were and I was not even scared. I was overjoyed. It was not until after the war that I learned the pilots never had any idea where we were located. We were just lucky.

I found out later that an empty shell casing that was part of a fire bomb had fallen and hit one of the barracks. A young man named Pete Mendola was playing his guitar. Someone asked him to play, "Home Sweet Home." Pete had just started to play when that empty shell casing fell through the roof and right down between Pete's thumb and the palm of his hand. Pete lost his thumb and one finger and would never be able to play the guitar again. However, Pete Mendola was very lucky to still be alive and able to tell about it. I feel a greater power protected us and we just never realized it. When that long raid was over we were rousted out to fight fires. When the sun came up we saw devastation everywhere. Just a building standing here and there. I wanted to shout a great big loud "Hallelujah." I felt good knowing I was right for a change. The Japanese were going to pay a big price for attacking America.

I looked toward the bay. We had launched a ship the day before that was not quite ready. The electrical work had to be completed. The bombs had sunk that ship before it could make its maiden voyage. Then I looked toward the shipyards and saw they had been destroyed. I wanted to shout another "Hallelujah." Although I could not help but hope the good people who had given us salt had escaped.

Chapter Thirteen

I WAS ASSIGNED TO WORK IN THE KITCHEN AGAIN and made boss of the morning shift. We were already starving, and after that raid the Japanese cut our food rations in half. I had no idea how I was to make so little go so far and feed so many.

When I first came to that camp, there were almost a thousand men. At that time we had maybe seven hundred and we had not been there but a few months. Unfortunately, things had deteriorated so much that it was a death sentence to be taken to the hospital. The hospital was the last place you wanted to go if you were sick. Consequently we had many men so ill they could hardly walk. About a half-mile from our barracks there was an old warehouse where three horses were kept along with some old rubber tires. When that warehouse caught fire, two horses burned up. The third horse ran from the fire toward the river and got bogged down in a mud hole about a hundred feet from the bank.

The Japanese formed work parties and took many prisoners out to help gather the dead so they could be cremated. Three days had passed since the night of that big raid. One of the work parties came across those two dead horses. In those three days the horses had swelled up with their legs stuck straight up in the air. The hair and the hoofs had been burned off them. Those prisoners were so hungry they yanked and broke off pieces of meat and ate those horses right then and there. They were like starving vultures gorging themselves over the carcass of a prize kill.

On the fourth day another work party found the other horse stuck in the mud and he was still alive. The horse had all his hair burned off and his nose was swelled up bigger than the top of his head. The horse was suffering something terrible. The Japanese guard in charge was kind enough to shoot the horse and put him out of his misery. The guard told the men if the camp doctor said the horse was still edible, we could have him to eat.

The doctor went out and checked the horse. He told us the horse was all right to eat. Everyone who was not out searching for the dead, fighting fires, or cleaning things in general, in other words everyone still in camp, volunteered to be the butcher of that poor old horse. They thought that by being a butcher they would get something extra to eat. Finally it was decided who would go and several men departed to saw off the head of that horse with a little knife no bigger than a pocket knife. They took a small two-wheeled cart in which to carry him back to camp.

About an hour later they returned. The horse was in pieces with his head tucked between his hind legs. He was covered with that stinking mud and stunk worse than a skunk. Just the sight of that horse made me sick and I walked away. I felt sorry for all the animals caught up in the middle of man's conflict with each other. The animals were the silent sufferers and casualties of war.

The men started to skin the horse with vegetable knives. Nobody knew what they were doing yet everybody was trying and hoped to get a little extra portion. They worked for over an hour on that horse before they finally got the hide off.

When I returned the nicest aroma was emiting from the kitchen and the room was full of men. Everyone was busy. I could not help but smile because it was my job to get the kitchen help out of bed every morning such as it was. I always had trouble getting the guys up. They would moan and groan about it, but I did not have a choice. If the Japanese guards came along and caught me short-handed I would get beaten. I had to get them up. Yet that morning they were all in the kitchen. I mean every man who worked in the kitchen on every shift. You could not get anyone to leave. Everyone wanted a piece of that horse.

It was hard to believe that horse could smell so good when it smelled so bad earlier. Several of the men could not wait for the roasts cooking in the ovens and tore a piece off and put it in the firebox to cook it quickly. Larry Wah Bing Ching, who had worked in the kitchen on Wake Island, walked over to me with a real nice looking piece of meat and said, "Ain't you going to cook a piece of this meat?"

"No Larry. I cannot eat horse."

"Why in the hell not?"

"I raised horses and they have always been my friends."

"I'll bet you raised cattle, too, but you wouldn't turn down a steak if we had any," Larry said.

"I was never close to cows as I was horses," I replied and yet I was sure tempted. That horsemeat smelled good and I was hungry. I kept thinking about Cherry. I will always regret not taking Cherry with me that last time. I received a letter from June about six months later that the man who worked for him had forgotten to close the door to the storage area where the grain was stored. Cherry got in there and ate too much grain, foundered, and died.

When Larry mentioned cows, that sparked an old memory. I remembered when Dad had to shoot three hundred head of cattle and told to leave them for the buzzards. I thought about how many steaks I could get from three hundred cows and my mouth watered just thinking about a big beef steak. Larry interrupted my thoughts when he kept insisting I take a little taste.

"If I take a taste, I will want to eat the whole horse–I am so hungry."

Larry would not stop until I took a taste, so to appease him I tasted it. It was so good I could not resist cutting off a piece and putting it in the firebox, too. However, I felt very guilty because the guys outside were not getting as much to eat as we were in the kitchen. It was taking food out of their mouths, so I did not eat anymore.

It was not until the war ended when I asked the head cook why he always asked for me to work in the kitchen. And I am proud to say he told me that I was one of the few men he could depend upon not to eat more than his share. I felt good about that.

A few days later the Japanese came in at night and lined us up. We were marched about four miles through town. There were burnt buildings, tin, and junk lying everywhere. The area looked worse than anything I had ever seen. I do not think an earthquake or anything Mother Nature could have done could have caused a more perfect job of destruction. I silently shouted a big "hooray" under my breath. It may not have been the Christian way, but it seemed so appropriate at the time. I yearned for revenge. I wanted the Japanese to suffer like I had. I wanted them to die like so many of my friends had died.

Then I would remember the kind heart of that elderly hauncho and the people who had helped us when they could. I realized that all Japanese people were not cruel. As in all conflicts of war, it was their leaders who led them into destruction. They had little to say about it.

We were put on a little old train, a little puffer belly that looked very small in comparison to the steam engines I was used to riding back in the United States. I could not help but long for the sound of an American locomotive. I never knew of anything more touching to the soul as the melancholy moan of the whistle on a steam locomotive of that era. You could hear it for miles as it echoed across the valley. It was a beckoning call for all those who possessed a restless spirit. And the *clickity-clak* of the wheels rolling on the rails was a hobo's lullaby. I remembered the excitement I had when I rode the rails with Coley. I kept the men entertained with my stories about being a hobo.

COLEY AND I KNEW BETTER than to flash any money when bumming around so we sewed it up in the cuff of our pants and kept five dollars in our pocket for spending money. No way would we let the other hobos know we had any money or we would be taking chances of being robbed. On one adventure Coley and I caught a freight train going east. There was one hobo ridding with us, and every time that train stopped he would get off and bum something to eat. He never missed a time and always returned with something tasty. Coley and I decided we would try that and save what money we had for something else other than food.

Coley and I were warned several times about the railroad bulls at Green River. The hobos told us the bulls were generally very tough on bums they caught there. We were not sure what train to take to miss Green River. Coley and I were not very worried and we ended up taking whatever train was leaving at the time we were ready to go.

The train began slowing as it labored up a long sloping hill. We could hear the heavy puffing of the steam locomotive way ahead. Black Rock Canyon was directly below, and Coley and I looked anxiously for any signs of water there. We thought if we saw any water we would jumped off and get a drink and catch the next train going through.

The train unexpectedly pulled onto a siding and stopped. A railroad bull appeared from out of nowhere. He was wearing a six-shooter that hung low on his hip like he might have to out-draw somebody. He took out his gun and started walking right down that train and made every hobo get off, threatening to shoot anyone who did not do exactly as he ordered.

That bull literally herded sixteen of us toward the end of the train waving his six-shooter around and shouting orders. Coley and I tried keeping up as we walked on the ties, and it was not easy trying to keep in step with a bunch of stumble bums.

The railroad bull told us he was going to teach us a lesson that we would not soon forget. He kept us standing in the hot sun until close to two o'clock in the afternoon and the temperature was close to a hundred degrees. A train going east passed and we were all tempted to make a run for it, except I do believe that bull would have shot us if we tried.

As soon as the train going east had passed, the whistle blew from the locomotive pulling the train we were on and it started to huff and puff and the cars jerked and slowly started to roil. When the caboose came by the railroad bull jumped on. How we wished he would have missed those ladder steps and fallen but he did not. I yelled, "How far is town?"

"Twenty miles," the bull shouted as he kept getting farther away.

"What direction?" I yelled.

In a very superior attitude the bull was laughing when he shouted, "Go west young man. Go west."

Coley and I watched as the train pulled out of sight. Some men began jogging toward town and some just walked very fast. There was one old man who was having a hard time of it and left behind. Coley and I decided to stay with him and make sure that he made it.

We walked slowly and finally made it to the top of the hill. Those men who had started out trotting were sitting under a tree soaking up the shade. They were exhausted. We could see the little town about five or six miles away as the crow flies. Coley, the old man, and I just kept on walking slowly, leaving those trotters behind. Pretty soon we passed those men who were walking fast. They had stopped to rest, too. Coley and I could see that the old man needed to rest so we told him to sit for awhile in the shade with the others and we would come back with water to get him.

Coley and I continued walking at a leisurely pace and we were the first to reach town. We had to laugh about that. It reminded us of the old story of the tortoise and the hare. We bought two quarts of cold buttermilk and gulped them down. When we finished we washed out those quart bottles and filled them with water. We started walking back to meet the old man.

Coley and I met the old man about two miles out of town and never was a person more glad to see us than he was. He drank one quart of water right there and poured part of the other over his head. He thanked us over and over again for returning to help him.

Coley and I could not believe what those other hobos were drinking as we passed them. When they had reached the stock yards they were so thirsty they just brushed back that mossy stuff on top of the water in the watering toughs that was for cattle and drank that old dirty water. God only knew what was in it.

It was difficult for me to believe that a man could be so inhuman to other men over a train ride. I am sure if the railroad had given that railroad bull permission, he would have enjoyed shooting us.

Coley and I were to learn that was really a tough town for hobos. We had even a harder time getting out of town without being thrown into jail. Once you were incarcerated you were sent out on work details and it could be several weeks before you ever gained your freedom again. Coley and I decided to hitch-hike. That, too, was another story.

Another time Coley and I decided to jump off a train at Ogden, Utah. It was after dark when the train began slowing before coming into the rail yard As the train slowed, Coley was on one side of the car and I was on the other. I jumped first and I thought Coley had jumped from the other side. When I hit the ground, I heard Coley yell my name. I thought something had happened and he had changed his mind about getting off. I hurriedly got to my feet and ran to get back on the train. I was barely able to catch the ladder of a freight car in the dark. I stood on that ladder and hung on with all the strength I had and rode into the rail yard. When the train came to a stop I jumped off again and started looking for Coley. There was a lot of hobos on that train and when Coley was not among them I started worrying.

What if Coley had jumped and the train ran over him? Maybe that is what had happened when he called out to me. Maybe he needed help. I started running back up the tracks on the edge of panic, calling for Coley as

I ran. It was a black night and I could not see anything. It was so dark I probably would not have been able to find him if I had tripped over him.

I must have walked back at least two miles before I stopped. I knew it was not any farther than that when I had jumped off the train. I was so upset I abandoned all restraint and threw myself down and pounded the ground with my fists. I felt so helpless and I was so very tired I decided to stay right there overnight next to the railroad tracks. In the morning I would continue my search. I dreaded the coming of daylight and the possibility of finding Coley's body parts strewed along the railroad tracks. I finally fell into a sound but troubled sleep. All too often hobos were killed while trying to get on or off a train.

I remembered one time we were in a coal car with several other hobos. It was so crowded that three hobos had to sit on the back of it. The engineer put on the brakes and started up again. When he took up the slack, it caused a big jerk and one of those fellows sitting on the back fell off and the wheels ran over him. We were all afraid of the railroad bulls. They would probably think one of us pushed him and none of us wanted to stick around to answer questions. So like fleas on a dead dog, every hobo in that coal car jumped off, including Coley and me. The highway ran alongside the train tracks, and we ran for it as fast as we could. There were hobos strung out along that highway for a mile. It looked as if a hobo convention had just let out.

I was still sleeping when something bit me on the lip. It hurt so much I jumped up and looked for whatever it was that bit me, but to this day I have no idea what it was. My lip swelled up clear out to the end of my nose. I looked gruesome.

It was breaking day so I started walking slowly along the tracks toward the railroad yard investigating anything that looked suspicious. I was so glad when I never found any body parts. I was so discouraged I sat on a bench just staring at the ground. I did not know what I should do next.

"What is the matter kid?" a voice said.

I looked up to see an engineer and a brakeman who had just finished their shift. My lip was so swelled it was difficult for me to talk. I told them about losing my brother and how worried I was that he may have been run over. I added that I did not know what to do or where I should go.

"You come with us," the engineer insisted and I followed them like a lost puppy. They insisted I clean up in their bath house before getting something to eat. I must admit I sure enjoyed taking a hot shower. The engineer told me that he was going to tell the head bull my story and assured me that the head bull would help me find my brother.

The engineer bought breakfast for me and then took me to the head bull. After hearing my story the bull put me on a train going to Ogden. The sun was well up when the train pulled out. When I looked over at another train just coming in, I saw Coley sitting on top of one of the cars. I yelled at the top of my lungs and Coley turned and looked at me. I motioned for him to get off. I watched him climb down the ladder and jump off. The same bull that put me on the train reached out and grabbed Coley. I waved in acknowledgment that the man he had was my brother and I knew he would keep Coley there until I could get back. That railroad bull was a real nice fellow compared to some.

I caught another freight back and joined Coley as soon as I could. By that time the swelling in my lip was abating and I was beginning to look human again.

Then another time Coley and I were riding a flatcar that developed a hot box when the lubricating oil ran out and the box caught fire when the bearings overheated. Coley and I could hardly breathe for the thick black smoke that boiled into the air. We could feel the heat from that wheel bearing, and we jumped off when it burst into flames. Coley and I had to walk for miles across dry land and a lot of Indians were living there near the salt cities. They stored water in crock jars and water bags and hung them from trees with gunny sacks tied around them to help keep the water cool. Although Coley and I were thirsty I remembered the encounter I had at Yuma, and I was not about to drink any of their water without permission.

Unlike the Indians at Yuma, these Indians came out and greeted us with a smile. They seemed to know what we needed and let us drink all the water we wanted. Coley and I thanked them and walked to the railroad tracks to catch the first freight train out. Coley and I never had any problems after that and for that we were thankful. My story ended when the train stopped and we were herded like cattle to our new home.

I COULD NOT EVEN, IMAGINE a POW camp being worse than the one we just left, but the next camp, called Aomori or Amori, I am not sure of the spelling, was the roughest, the toughest, and most inhuman camp of all. I was still there when the war was over. Several men who did not die lost their minds in that camp.

The Japanese commander was a cold, uncaring individual. He wore his power like a Samurai wears his sword, and he left most of the discipline measures up to a guard who was pure evil. He was a maniac, a madman who derived pleasure in torturing and watching the suffering of men who could not defend themselves.

There were two two-story barracks on one side of the camp and about a hundred yards from those was a three-story barrack. The kitchen and guard house were on another side, and the center of the compound was bare like a parade ground of sorts. That was where the Japanese had their flag flying and the commander of the camp gave his speeches.

Every biting insect that crawled or sucked blood lived inside the walls of those barracks. The little straw mattresses we slept on were loaded with fleas, bed bugs, and lice. Within a few days we had little red dots all over us where we had been bitten. The fleas and bed bugs were eating us alive. It was so bad we could not sleep at night, so every other night I gave my blanket to the man next to me so he could wrap up and get some sleep and he in turn gave me his blanket every other night so I could get some sleep. Everybody took turns with their bunkie next to them, otherwise nobody got any sleep.

To our astonishment the Japanese began paying us for our labor. We received two cents for an eighteen-hour day. With all that Japanese yen, we gambled. If a man was lucky he could win enough to bribe some food from the Japanese mess sergeant.

During the summer that mean guard would make us stand out in the hot sun and hold a fence post over our head with both arms. Even men who were in good shape could not have taken that treatment for very long, and we were so weak from malnutrition we could not do it for very long at all. When we could not hold the post up any longer and dropped it, that Japanese guard hit you with his rifle butt and made you stand some more. When finally you were so exhausted you fell to your knees, he would kick you unconscious, then throw water on you to bring you to and make you go through it again. That went on until he became tired of the game or you died. He derived pleasure from giving punishment and seeing just how much pain a man could take before passing out or going crazy or surrendering to death.

Needless to say we hated him with a passion. Being a coward at heart, he always surrounded himself with plenty of protection. There was not a prisoner there who did not want to kill him and prayed that he should die a very painful death.

The Japanese were terrible about losing their tempers. And once they started hitting you for whatever the reason, they would not stop. They seemed to build up a rage, a temper tantrum that turned into a vicious frenzy. And you never knew whether you were going to be beaten severely, kicked to death, or stuck with a bayonet and killed. Everyday of life in that camp was like living a game of Russian roulette. To keep up our morale every year, we made up little verses that rhymed about our situation. One was:

> The war will be through in forty-two
> We'll be free in forty-three
> No more war in forty-four
> Home alive in forty-five

One evening I was on my way to the kitchen and I saw two guards beating a friend of mine who was mentally sick. They had beaten him senseless. I could not stand it and I went over to them. I told the guards my friend was sick and had lost his mind. If they did not stop they were going to kill him. They stopped beating my friend and transferred their attention to me. They started beating on me, and I thought they would never quit until I was dead.

They beat me with those bamboo sticks that were split at the end. Every time that stick came down across my back and head it felt like several scissors cutting me apart. I put my hands up to protect my face, but I was hit with a rifle butt. I fell to my knees and they beat the hide off the back of my neck, half my face, and clipped the hair off my head. My scalp had so many deep cuts you would have thought I had been scalped. I was a bloody mess.

Finally they told me to get up and get back to the kitchen and never meddle in Japanese business again. I had to leave my friend lying unconscious on the ground, but at least they had stopped beating him, too. Two prisoners were allowed to carry my friend back to his barracks. I was glad to get back to that kitchen. I thought for awhile I was at the end of my life.

On one hand I did not want to work in the kitchen because the men always thought you were eating their share of the food and hollered at you all the time about that. An invisible wall of indifference stood between us. Even though I knew I was not doing anything wrong, I felt like an outcast. And yet on the other hand, working there undoubtedly saved my life. In spite of that I wanted out and the head cook named Gancy would not let me leave. So I asked him why.

"You are as honest as anyone I can get in here and you care about the men. If you want to get home someday you will stay where you're at," Gancy said.

I could not argue with him on that point. And I am proud to say I am probably the only cook in history who lost weight working in the kitchen.

Chapter Fourteen

THE MEN WERE MADE TO WALK TO WORK IN THE STEEL MILLS over a mile away. Since I worked in the kitchen, I would watch them march away and I would pray for their safety and our rescue from that agony of life and living hell.

They walked like men without hope, their heads lowered, their shoulders stooped and rounded from the heavy labor. They were walking skeletons from lack of food. Dark circles had formed under empty eyes from the lack of rest. They were sick in body and spirit. It is truly amazing what the human body can withstand to stay alive.

The planes bombed that area frequently, and again, no bombs ever came near our barracks. Even though I was sure the Americans knew exactly where we were, I worried about a stray bomb or an empty shell that might miss its mark, especially after what happened to Pete Mendola.

I must tell you about the old antique fire engine we had. It was the kind that had to be pulled by horses that you have seen in the old silent movies. It was made with a long wooden bar on each side. It took three men on each side to pump up and down to get any water.

The camp was next to a river, so when the air-raid sirens blasted, I was in the detail of men in charge of opening the gates and getting the suction hose into the river so there would be water to pump, while another detail of men stood in readiness at the side of that old engine to pump water should the camp get bombed and catch fire.

That mean Japanese guard was in charge of us on fire detail. If we did not have the gates open, the suction hose in the river, and the fire engine ready to go by the time he got there, we would get beaten. If we did have the gates open, the suction hose in the river, and the fire engine ready to go we would get beaten for not waiting for him. It was a no-win situation and we knew that. He used any excuse to beat us. He also had a German iron helmet that he wore during air raids. That helmet must have weighed five pounds.

One night the sirens went off and just kept blowing. It was quite a weird sound if you had never heard it. Despite the volume, it was like living next to a railroad. Pretty soon you never hear the trains. We had been through those air raids so many times it was routine for us. We slowly hauled out to hook up the fire hoses. We waited five minutes or so for that mean guard and he was not in sight. We decided it was best to get prepared. We had everything ready to go when Satan's underling arrived. I thought he was going to have a heart attack from the fit he had. He did everything but lie on the ground and kick his feet into the air. It was a sight to behold. He was plenty mad at us over nothing and had us line up against the wall. I thought for a moment he was going to shoot us and put us out of our misery. All of us were so tired and beaten down we did not care anymore what happened.

He held the German helmet with both hands and came down as hard as he could with it over the head of the first man. I was about fifteenth in line and I did not want to see it coming so I closed my eyes. I could hear him hit each man with that helmet. Each head he hit made a different sound. A hard thump, a high pitch blow, a loud impact that echoed a cracked skull. I could not help but wonder what tone my skull was going to make. As he came nearer I tried not to show fear.

If you tried to dodge his blow it only made him more furious and he would hit you again. If you fell he loved to kick you unconscious. I opened my eyes for only a moment to see when it was my turn and he was standing in front of me. I dodged when I saw that helmet coming down. It was just a natural reaction. He hit me again as hard as he could across the side of my head and broke my eardrum. If we were not rescued soon, I knew I was not long for this world under such extreme conditions and brutal treatment. I was not physically up to it. At that time I weighed only eighty-six pounds. I had survived five months under that maniac when one day at about noon, the routine changed. We watched the guards fall out of the guard house and stand with rifles at attention. We had several men in that guard house and I prayed they were not preparing a firing squad. Then the Japanese National Anthem began playing without a reason. I had heard it several times before. Every time they won a big battle they would play that over the radio.

When the music stopped the guard let our men out of the guard house. A few minutes later the gates opened and the men came marching back from working in the steel mills. There were a lot of Korean prisoners there, and they told us the war was over–American tanks were in the streets of Tokyo. It was not true that American tanks were in the streets of Tokyo, but it was true that the war was over. However, we were still under guard.

That night the Japanese commander left the compound with his briefcase under his arm. We still did not know what was going on. Although under guard, we were left alone. We did not black out any windows that night and we could talk openly about everything and we were not made to be quiet.

The next day the Japanese commander returned and we were marched out to the center of the parade grounds. The commander got up on a platform and told us the fighting had ceased, but peace had not yet been signed and the Japanese might start fighting again. We still had to obey all the rules. You could tell he hated having to admit defeat. We were all hoping he would commit suicide.

In spite of the order given when that Japanese commander said the fighting was over, some of the men broke ranks and took it upon themselves to catch that mean guard. That guard took off like his butt was on fire. Unfortunately the men were in such poor condition they could not catch him even though they chased him out of the compound for quite a ways. If justice truly had been served, he should have had to suffer terrible pain and death. We never thought very much of that commander either for letting such a madman have his way like he did with the prisoners.

After the men were brought back and order was restored, we retreated to the barracks to talk among ourselves. Punishment and beatings had ceased and for that we were thankful. Of course that mean guard was never seen again. That night we had to black out the windows again and we were not allowed to talk or make any noise. We still had very short rations and other than not having to work, our living conditions had not changed at all.

The next day we were lying around camp wondering what was going to happen to us, when a two-seated Japanese fighter airplane flew over and started circling around and around in shorter circles. The plane was flying so low we could see the two men inside quite plainly. The pilot in the back seat kept pointing down to the camp to the pilot in the front. After a couple more circles they flew away. That caused much confusion among us. We did not know what to make of it and there were many speculations that maybe the war was continuing.

The following day a truck delivered several eight-feet-long boards about an inch thick to the camp. The Japanese commander told us to paint them yellow and nail them to the roof. The boards were to spell out P.W. We found out later that all prison camps were supposed to be marked like that or in a similar fashion, and the Japanese had not followed the rules of war.

We had no more finished doing that when we heard several airplanes coming in from a distance. Six Grumman fighters flew over doing barrel rolls and all kinds of tricks. We quickly wrote on the ground with white lime, FOOD, SMOKES. Those pilots threw out what cigarettes they had and a few candy bars. Some of those candy bars were half eaten, but we did not care. We had not had such a treat in years.

Seven hundred men, give or take a few were watching those little planes with their hearts in their throats. Seven hundred men were all crying like babies. Tears were flowing over their cheeks dripping off their chins. Some had fallen to their knees in thankfulness.

One plane flew in exceptionally low and dropped a note. He wrote they were from the aircraft carrier *Enterprise* and they would be back tomorrow. With that revelation the men went wild. Some celebrated with shouts of joy and some celebrated in quiet meditation of disbelief for they could not speak without crying. On the same day six Grumman fighters flew over later in the evening. Then we heard bigger planes that sounded like bombers. One man yelled, "Oh my God. The war has started again." We ran outside to see two torpedo bombers flashing signal lights. We had a few navy men who could read those signals and told us to get inside the barracks. The planes wanted to make a drop.

Those planes came in so low the motors were deafening and the noise vibrations shook the barracks as if we were in an earthquake. They dropped several sea-bags filled with K-rations. There was enough for half a K-ration per man. Those K-rations were more than just a survival kit. It brought us a little bit of the USA with a few cigarettes, a peanut butter bar, and several sticks of gum. Even though it was dark we marched into the kitchen and told the Japanese mess sergeant we wanted some rice.

"I cannot do that. I will get in big trouble with the commander," he replied in broken English.

"He does not have anything more to say about it," I said.

"Commander never told me," the Japanese sergeant replied.

"Those are American planes flying overhead. Nobody is shooting at them. They are dropping supplies. Do you really think the Japanese are in control?" I pointed out.

The Japanese mess sergeant had always been a pretty good fellow for the position he was in and I assured him that we were going to let the Americans know he had been as fair as he could be under the circumstances.

"Why are we talking to him? Let's get what we want. To hell with him," one of the other men shouted.

So we took what we wanted. We had every pot that we could find in that kitchen steaming with rice. In those K-rations were cans of ham pate about the size of a can of tuna. We took a gallon of rice and added a can of ham pate to it. We were so starved that the rice tasted gourmet and four men would wipe out a gallon of rice. We ate so much that night that most of us made ourselves sick.

I could not sleep that night. I waited for the sunrise like a little kid waiting up to get a glimpse of Santa Claus. I could only wonder what was coming next. I could not help but hope that somebody would come and send us home to family and loved ones. I wondered if Dad still had the ranch at

Paskenta. I was looking forward to riding a horse and herding cattle again. I remembered the last time I herded cattle. What a awful time I had of it.

DAD WANTED TO MOVE FOUR hundred head to the summer range as soon as possible, and I experienced a real old-fashioned cattle drive. The morning we saddled up to drive those cattle to the summer range had all the semblance of an old western movie. I was quite excited about everything in general and anxious to get started. I thought about Cherry and wished I had my horse there. Dad and Red led the way while Coley, Skeet, and I followed.

We drove the cattle across the Grindstone to Log Springs, which was twenty some odd miles away. The Grindstone was several conically shaped mounts that rose sharply above the surrounding rolling hills and were topped by jagged rock outcroppings that protruded in high relief over sheer cliffs.

In between we had to cross a section called Poison Glade, then a series of rolling treeless hills that looked like they had been carpeted. We crossed Tom's Creek and rode over to Black Butte. And what a bad time we had of it with the bulls wanting to fight each other every step of the way.

I was captivated by the sheer beauty of the locality. It had been a wet year so everything was lush and green. The area was so lovely and so different from that which I had known in New Mexico. I had not yet seen the region in the summer when everything turned brown and it was so hot you did not need a stove to cook your food. Just set it out in the sun and everything turned to jerky. Everything was going along splendidly so I relaxed my guard. That is when one bull got himself turned around and charged another bull. Before I could stop them from fighting, the bulls knocked several cows over a steep cliff. It was a terrible loss. Dad told me as soon as the cattle were across Tom's Creek I was to return to that ravine the next day and rescue any cows that had survived the fall.

Crossing Tom's Creek was not easy either. The water was running high and fast. The cows could get across, but the calves washed down stream if we did not keep them on the upper side of the cows. Red, Coley, and I were real good at roping and were kept busy roping and dragging those little calves upon the bank. By the time we finished, all of us, including the horses, were exhausted so we made camp and stayed the night.

The next morning I left to rescue those cows that had fallen over the cliff the day before. I rode back across the creek and down that narrow trail to the bottom of that mount and entered the ravine. I found four cows dead. I could not tell if the fall had killed them or not since the bears had gotten to them. I found six others scattered throughout the draw. It was tough going getting those cows out of there. I had to ride through thick brush that grew in abundance along the creek and at times through the creek itself over large rocks. It was terribly hard on my horse and the cows. Once I had the cows safely upon the trail, they did not want to go over that narrow pathway again. I had to rope the lead cow and literally drag her behind my horse. When I did that, the other cows followed. When camp finally came into view, I was overjoyed. I was tired and hungry. I had ridden well over twenty miles that day.

There is nothing like sitting around the campfire after a hard day's ride with family and friends. Lying under a star-filled sky with the pacifying sound of the night's breezes blowing through the trees is an experience everyone should have at least once in a lifetime.

The first time I saw Black Butte I was surprised to see a large table-top mountain. I had expected to see a big conical black mountain of sorts. When we were getting close to the end of the trail drive, I hurt my foot and it needed medical attention. Dad told me to return to the ranch-house and have Iva doctor it as soon as possible. I hated having to leave everyone and return to the ranch alone, yet I did not want to take any chances of infection setting in, so I sadly told everyone I would see them back at the ranch.

My big toe swelled and I could not put my boot on, so I rode my horse wearing only one boot. When you are riding a horse downhill, the horse walks stiff-legged and makes ridding very difficult. Even though I had my foot resting in a stirrup, I could feel every step of that horse. Once in a while, the stirrup would accidently hit that toe and I grit my teeth to keep from yelling the pain was so intense. I felt every heartbeat in that big toe. It was a miserable all-day ride, and it was well after dark when I finally arrived at the ranch.

Not wanting to disturb anyone, I tried being quiet when I hobbled into the house. Iva heard me fumbling around in the kitchen and came to see what was going on. She made me sit while she found a pan for me to soak my foot in salt water. She put creosote on it and I thought I was on fire. For the next week I lived the life of a semi-invalid. Fortunately my toenail grew back in time.

Once the cattle were settled on the summer range there was not that much to do, so three days later Dad, Red, Coley, and Skeet returned. Every once in a while, Red and Skeet would ride to the mountains to check on the cattle. That was fine for them because Red worked for Dad and Skeet was still living at home. But Coley and I were supposed to be living on our own so we needed money coming in. Roy came to the ranch every once in a while to play cowboy and see how things were progressing. When Roy realized that Coley and I needed money, he told us he would pay us a hundred dollars for a thousand cedar posts. Coley and I agreed.

We armed ourselves with a crosscut saw, a splitting wedge, an axe, and everything we thought we might need. We took Dad's flatbed truck and headed to the mountains towards Covolo. We worked like two lumberjacks cutting down trees, splitting logs, and sawing posts. We camped out and came home about every three days with a truckload of posts. It took Coley and I three weeks to cut a thousand posts and haul them back to the ranch.

When Roy returned to the ranch he paid us the hundred dollars. Once Coley and I had money in our pockets, it was like giving us a green light to the open road.

"The open road," I repeated out loud to myself. Those were beautiful words. One of the men heard me and shook me to bring me back into reality. It was morning and he was warning me to come out of it. I told him thanks and not to worry; I was all right.

ABOUT THAT TIME WE HEARD the unmistakable sound of the motors of the B-29. We knew immediately what kind of plane that was because we had seen and heard hundreds of them fly over the last few months during bombing raids.

That B-29 was painted blue and silver. When it flew over, we read PW SUPPLIES written on the under side of the wing. The plane flashed lights and again we were told to go inside–they were going to drop supplies. We watched that B-29 with all the attention a lowly private gives to a general. The plane made a big circle to gain altitude and flew back. We watched the bomb-bay doors open wide. And you never saw such a pretty picture in your life. Every color of parachute in the world except black fell out of that plane. We could see what looked like little beer kegs hanging on those parachutes. When they hit the ground, it was two fifty-gallon steel drums welded together and big sacks the size of cotton sacks were also attached.

The barrels were filled with chocolate, condensed milk, coffee, medicine, cigarettes, gum, and split pea soup–lots of split pea soup. There was everything we needed. We immediately fixed split pea soup and again gorged ourselves to the point that our stomachs hurt. And it was pure euphoria to sit back and enjoy an American cigarette after eating. And the aroma of fresh coffee that filled the air smelled better than flowers in springtime. If those barrels had had a few dancing girls, our day would have been complete.

There were two hundred fifty pair of army shoes in those sacks. We were barefooted and desperate for shoes. We spent all that day dividing those shoes up until we got down to a half a shoe.

After having your body and mind starved for such a long time, not only is the body weak, you cannot think properly and you do silly things. After the third drop I not only was wearing shoes, I had ten pairs tied together and strung around my neck. I wore myself out carrying around those army shoes. They weighed almost as much as I did. Finally it dawned on me. What in the hell was I doing? I did not need ten pair of army shoes. I was going home soon.

Everyone carried extra shoes around their necks at that time, and we all came to the same conclusion at the same time. So we threw those extra shoes in the storage room where the rice had been stored. We had just about eaten all the rice anyway.

For ten days that B-29 made a drop of the same thing. When we left that camp on the first of September, I think we each had about two hundred pairs of shoes and an equal amount of cartons of cigarettes. What a dilemma we had. No way could we carry all those shoes. But not one carton of cigarettes was left behind.

All of us talked about burning the barracks before we left. After so many years of being told what to do and when to do it, we were so excited about leaving for home we forgot all about setting those barracks afire.

Japanese guards escorted us to the train. What a difference in their attitude. They could not do enough to help us in every way. It is a wonder I could not have heard my bones rattle as I made my way to the train. I was nothing but a walking skeleton with a thin layer of skin holding my bones together, so to speak.

It was early morning when we boarded the train. Knowing I was on the way home seemed almost too good to be true. For days a sense of unreality stayed with me, as if I were dreaming. There were times when I would pinch myself just to make sure I was not.

Even though it was wonderful to be back on a train, the Japanese passenger car was nothing more than a cattle car with wooden seats. I leaned back in the seat and tried to let my body relax. I enjoyed the movement of the train car as it swayed from side to side. I listened to the familiar melodious beat of the wheels as they rolled along the tracks and the sound brought back a number of pleasant memories. I breathed a big sigh of contentment and fell in and out of cat naps.

We rode all day with little to munch on except whatever we had left over from K-rations, some chocolate and peanut bars and gum. The train stopped twice for about ten minutes and we were not allowed to get off. Nobody wanted to get off anyway. We were so far north it was after dark when we pulled into Tokyo. The Salvation Army and the Red Gross had hot coffee and donuts waiting for us. Never did a donut taste so good.

There were mine sweepers still clearing mines from Tokyo bay. They were blowing up mines and it gave us quite a show. It was fascinating to watch those mines blow up and the water spring way up in the air just like what you see in the movies.

I stepped from the train and the military had everything roped off. It was so reassuring to at last see American marines standing guard. There were several little canvas tents about the size of a small bathroom that were equipped with an X-ray machine. All of us had to go through there and have a chest x-ray. Many of the men were sent straight to hospital ships that were sitting out in Tokyo bay. Ropes had been strung to make isles for us to follow. We had to line up and wait our turn before we found out which line to get into. Some men were standing in line waiting to be transported to airplanes and flown home. I was placed in a line to board a ship. It seemed every conveyance had been put into service to help evacuate the POW'S.

At last I was told to board the LST *Ozark*. As soon as I stepped on that ship, I felt I was half way home. Just getting my feet off Japanese soil made my spirits soar. I thought I would have a good supper that evening instead I had the same thing I had been having for the last ten days, split pea soup. I began to wonder about that. Needless to say in spite of being starved for so long, I was getting a little tired of split pea soup. The *Ozark* stayed in Tokyo Bay all night. The next morning we were given mush for breakfast. Again I was a disappointed. I had visions of ham and eggs, cold milk, and fresh fruit. After breakfast I walked upon deck. Tokyo Bay was full of activity. There were three white hospital ships and they looked so beautiful with big red crosses painted on each side. I could see the battleship *Missouri* anchored about half a mile from us. We waited there until the peace agreements were finalized.

After all the formalities of the peace signing had been observed, the *Ozark* pulled anchor. I will never forget about half way through the bay there was a Japanese soldier floating face down. The waves were whipping his arms and legs and made him look like he was swimming home. Seeing him gave me a terrible feeling. There was something about that Japanese soldier looking as though he was still trying to get home even after death, that will be forever branded in my mind. I could relate to that picture, and in my emotional state I broke down and cried for an hour. I could not help but wonder if his folks would ever find him. The *Ozark*, dropped anchor at Guam. I was put in the hospital there for ten days. I was kept on that same diet of mush in the morning and split pea soup for lunch and dinner. It is a wonder I had not turned green I had eaten so much split pea soup.

I could not believe it when several letters were delivered to me at Guam. Letters my family and friends had written long ago. I do not know if the Red Cross or the Japanese had held them, I only knew how happy I was at receiving them. In the early part of the war, once in a great while the Red Cross brought mail to the prisoners. But I never received any mail. I really thought I had not removed my name soon enough from that fatalities list on that bulletin board on Wake Island and my family probably thought I was dead. On the fourth day while I was in the hospital on Guam, the door to the ward I was in flew open and there was my friend who had lost his mind. I will not mention his name because he never wanted his family to know about that. He was in a wheel chair. He could not walk because he had athlete's foot so bad his feet were festered all over. His mental faculties had returned and he told me he was being flown home right away. He promised to call my folks and let them know I was in the hospital in Guam and that I was all right. I thanked him and we said goodbye. I wrote to him when I returned home and thanked him for letting my folks know I was all right. He never answered and I know he received my letter. I figured he was afraid I might mention what had happened to him, and he never wanted to continue the friendship so I never saw him again.

◁　◁　◁　◁　▷　▷　▷　▷

Chapter Fifteen

THE DAY BEFORE WE WERE TO LEAVE THE HOSPITAL a nurse came in and told us to follow her. There was a big quonset hut next to the hospital and they had tables set up inside that ran the full length of the building. All the POW'S were being given a farewell surprise party.

The tables were loaded with gourmet delicacies. Roasted meats of all kinds and bowls of mashed potatoes and gravies. Every vegetable you could possibly want was served, even peas. We took a seat and my eyes were glued to all that delicious-looking food. I could not hardly hold myself back from sneaking something from the table. A man announced over a loud speaker, "You are off your diet, so dive in."

And dive in we did. There was very little talking. Only the familiar sound of eating utensils could be heard as they softly collided against the bowls and plates. When we finished it was announced a store had been set up for us on the hospital grounds, and we did not have to pay for anything. I was really surprised to discover the store had everything we needed, such as underwear, sundries, razors, and blades. The only things we did not need were shoes and cigarettes.

To make that day perfect, the USO put on a show for us with movie stars and a well-known comedian named Charley Ruggles. After the show the stars told us they would be glad to sign autographs if we wanted them. All I had was some Japanese yen in my pocket that I had won, so I got all their autographs on that old money.

Before we left the hospital at Guam, the Red Cross gave each civilian five dollars. The marines received one hundred dollars and each navy man got three months' pay depending upon his rating at the time he was taken prisoner. My wonderful friend Gancy, who was a chief radio man and had been in the navy for twenty years, had received a sizable sum of money. He handed me a hundred dollar bill and said, "I know you like to gamble. When you get home you can send it to me at my New York address."

"Thanks Gancy. I will put your money to good use," I replied.

"Be careful. When those sailors see all the money you fellows have they are going to want to play poker. Do not lose it all at once," Gancy advised.

"Do not worry. You taught me pretty good," I replied and said goodbye to one of the greatest fellows it has been my pleasure to meet in this lifetime. Gancy was returning to Shanghai. Before the war he had married a white Russian and she was waiting for him there. I never understood just what the difference was between a white and a black Russian, especially when everyone referred to Russians as reds. I did not let things like that bother me, anyhow. The next morning we boarded the *Ozark* again and headed for Hawaii. The captain announced we would be at sea four days. I could not help but remember the last time I was in Honolulu, and I looked forward to being there again.

The cooks on the *Ozark* were wonderful to us. They announced that anytime we wanted a steak whether it be day or night they would fix it for us. We received the red carpet treatment all the way home with the end result being I was starting to feel pretty good, mentally, physically, and spiritually.

Gancy was right. Poker was King aboard ship. I was well aware I was not playing for match sticks or for rabbits and I was not playing with my brothers or good friends. I was playing with a bunch of guys who meant business and played for keeps. I knew I had to remember everything Gancy and my brothers ever taught me.

I played poker every day and I would have made Gancy proud. When we docked at Honolulu, I had over twelve hundred dollars. I was elated over the prospect of buying a new Buick when I returned home. I wanted a new Buick for as long as I could remember. When I left California to go to Wake Island in 1941, you could buy a new Buick loaded with everything for twelve hundred dollars.

We were told not to leave the ship because the *Ozark* was leaving Honolulu for San Francisco at two in the morning. I felt restless so I was given permission to walk around the harbor but warned not to get out of sight. Another fellow named Clayton Walcott walked with me and then another man joined us. I do not remember his name. We were walking as if we knew where we were going and a jeep drove by and slid to a stop.

"Hey you guys want a ride into Honolulu?" the driver yelled.

I looked at Clayton and he was looking at me. We both looked at the other guy and said, "Why not?"

It was still early in the evening and we celebrated and partied until midnight. When the clock struck twelve I told my buddies we better return to the ship and I called a taxi. The taxi took us to the harbor gate and let us out. I paid him and he drove away. When we started to enter the harbor gate, two marines pulled their guns on us. They would not let us through. We sure had not planned on anything like that happening.

I explained we were supposed to sail on the *Ozark* at two in the morning. One of the marines walked over to a telephone and called the ship. I thought for sure we were in deep trouble. On the contrary, a car was sent to the gate to pick us up and the marines escorted us to the *Ozark* and made sure we boarded that ship before they would leave. Since we were POWS and civilians we never caught hell. I would not want to do that if I were in the military or I would probably still be in the brig.

Because everyone was so anxious to get home, they complained how slow the *Ozark* was. I thought it was fast compared to the ship I had sailed on going to Hawaii the first time. The ship's crew entertained us by turning balloons loose and then shooting them down. They showed us how the newer guns worked in comparison to the older models. I played more poker and lost. I decided I needed a break so I rested for awhile. When I returned I won back eleven hundred dollars and decided to quit while I was ahead.

An interesting fact was pointed out to me while on the *Ozark*. All the importance that Japan put on Wake Island was wasted and never materialized simply because America perfected the long-range bomber and did not need Wake Island as a refueling stop. Wake Island was even more costly than the Japanese ever imagined to maintain. And many men died from malnutrition because the Japanese were not able to get supplies to Wake Island since America controlled the air and the sea. It would seem what goes around comes around.

I really enjoyed the boat trip to San Francisco. I was sure I must be the happiest man in the world just knowing I was going home. When I caught the first glimpse of the Golden Gate Bridge in the distance, I could not hold back the tears. I never realized how great a country I lived in until I lost it.

On the north bank white rocks spelled the words, WELCOME HOME BOYS. JOB WELL DONE. After reading that I had never been so moved. I got a big lump in my throat and I could not even speak. I was so emotionally taught I just stood there in awe trying desperately to hold back the sobs of joy and thankfulness. There was not a POW who was not teary eyed.

When the skyline of San Francisco came into view, I could not think of anything except I was at last home. I had survived the pit of hell and made it back in one piece. Once my feet were on California soil, I promised myself I would never leave the shores of California again. I reached down and grabbed some dirt. I smelled and kissed it. I told the fellows that even the dirt in California was worth its weight in gold.

We were assigned rooms in hotels all over San Francisco. Larry Wah Bing Ching from Hawaii, Cecil Strickland from Williams, California, Clayton Marcott, who was from the south, and me, all shared one room.

Taxis were waiting to take us to the hotel. As soon as I was settled in the hotel room, I thought about calling Dad and I decided not to. I hated Dad seeing me looking so puny. Besides I was still on an emotional roller coaster. Before I went home I wanted to go shopping for new western boots, a Stetson, and a pair of dress shoes. I needed something besides army shoes to wear. I would have liked new clothes, but I was so thin I knew anything I bought would be too small in a month or so.

Finding a shoe store was easy. Finding a pair of handmade western boots was not, so I had to settle for a pair of dress shoes. Larry was buying three pair and Cecil had two. When I started to pay for my shoes the salesman asked for a stamp.

"What stamp?" I replied.

"A stamp from your ration book," the salesman said.

"I do not have any ration book," I replied.

"What you are talking about?" Clayton added.

"Where have you guys been the last four years?" the salesman said.

"In a Japanese prison camp," I answered.

The salesman thought for a minute before telling us he did not think the country would have ration books much longer anyhow and sold us the shoes. When we returned to the hotel we were met by a young man who was there to give us a ration book. He apologized for being late.

We wanted to celebrate and went to a well-known bar where we knew several of our friends would be. I was having a real good time when the medic who worked with Shank walked in. I cannot remember his name. He knew me well enough to have Dad's address and telephone number in his pocket. I was always very lucky about people looking out for me. The medic walked over and asked if I had called my folks yet, and I told him no.

Without saying a word, he walked over to the telephone and called Dad. The medic returned and told me he had talked to Dad and my folks would be there in five hours. On one hand I was looking forward to seeing Dad again, and yet on the other I wished the medic had left that to me to do in my own time.

The four of us bought a bottle of liquor just before closing time and took our party to the hotel room. When Dad and Iva arrived the misgivings I had fostered about not wanting Dad to see me evaporated. I was never so glad to see anyone in my life. It was then that I knew the medic was right in calling them.

I offered my folks a drink and saw tears in Dad's eyes. I knew I must have looked a fright to him. After all, the last time he saw me I weighed one hundred sixty-five pounds and was in perfect health. When he looked at me now I barely weighed ninety pounds, had bad feet, bad back, broken ear drum, my hair had receded, and I was still suffering from the symptoms of malaria. I was in great shape for a young man of twenty-five.

Dad wanted to know about me. I told him I knew what hell was like and liberation came none too soon. Even though I worked in the kitchen, I knew I could not have lasted much longer. I asked Dad about my brothers and he told me Red and Coley were in the army and should be home any day, and Skeet had joined the Coast Guard.

We talked and Dad continued sipping one drink and then another. I did not know that Dad had been sick and he was not used to drinking. So in a short time Dad complained his stomach was upset and he began throwing up. That is when Iva told me he had not been feeling very well lately. I felt terrible for Dad. I tried getting another hotel room for Dad and Iva, but there was not one to be had. So I gave my bed to the folks and I bunked with Clayton.

When Dad was not feeling good by morning, I decided I better get him home. Larry Ching returned to Hawaii. Cecil and Clayton remained with me. We dropped Cecil off at his home in Williams, California. Clayton came home and stayed with me for two weeks before returning to Alabama.

Clayton liked the area so much he returned and lived out his life in California. He was a foreman of a big ranch near Yuba City, California, when he died. We remained friends all his life. Larry Ching visited and stayed two weeks with me many years later.

The relief and thankfulness of being home with family and friends was like a miracle to me; however, I will never be able to blank out the painful memories, the horror and the misery of those terrible years I spent in the Japanese prison camps.

I was invited to attend the trials for the accused Japanese war criminals to give testimony. Maybe I should have attended. I had mixed emotions about that. In today's world they would probably tell me I was suffering from emotional damage. All I knew was I did not want to leave home. I could not bring myself to leave the shores of California again. I was not ready to do that. I just wanted to forget.

I was not home very long before I met the girl of my dreams. She was beautiful. Her name was Norma McDermid. She had long, flowing, dark-brown hair that was as soft as cornsilk. When I looked into her dark-brown bedroom eyes, I knew in that moment that she was the one I wanted to spend the rest of my life with.

I will always remember the first time I took Norma home to meet the family. Red was home from the army and he had just received a letter from his girlfriend in Wyoming. She had been Red's girl for eight years. She gave Red an ultimatum—either he comes to get her right away to get married or forget the whole thing. If he decided not to get married, she never wanted to see Red again. After reading the letter, Red shook his head in disgust.

"What is the matter?" I asked.

"Read this," Red said and handed the letter to me. I read it and showed it to Norma.

"You would think a girl would give a fellow some time to make up his mind," Red said.

"She has waited eight years," I replied.

"That is quite awhile," Norma added.

Red did not go and get her so that romance ended. The love bug was busy that year. My sister Syble married Clifford Carrick, and one month later I married Norma. Then to everybody's surprise, Red married Dovey Carrick, Clifford Carrick's mother. Red stayed married one month and filed for divorce. Red returned to his horse and he never married again.

It was not until in the latter part of the 1980s that I could finally bring myself to leave California and travel to Wake Island once again. A special memorial was being given to the men who had fought and died on Wake Island. It was hard for me to believe I was there once again on that tiny piece of real estate, which I vowed I never wanted to see again. The island where I had lost so many friends, men who I would never see again. Men who died without ever fully knowing their sacrifice helped turn the tide of the Japanese onslaught. I considered I was standing on hallowed ground.

A prominent man gave a speech in honor of those men and his voice seemed to fade away as I was having a difficult time keeping my thoughts in the present. I kept drifting into the past as if it was yesterday, so much so my mind spiraled into a whirlpool of melancholy remembrances and it was all I could do to hold back the tears.

The sound of loud applause saved me from breaking down completely. The prominent man had finished his speech and the crowd was slowly dispersing. On one hand I was glad to have had the opportunity to visit Wake Island once more to have the chance to pay my last respects to those I had left behind so many years ago. A chance to stand in victory on the very spot where I was once taken prisoner and had experienced the most terrifying and sickening experiences of my life, which I have never been able to forget.

Then the time had come to say so long and return to California, the land that I loved. As I stepped up to the plane, I turned to say a goodbye to Wake Island forever and to my friends who had paid the ultimate price for the freedom we now enjoy. "All is well that ends well. I will see you later," I whispered, knowing that someday I, too, would have to pass through that unseen portal of this world into the next. I can only pray that my comrades know of the victory they helped achieve with the ending of World War II.

I turned again and stepped into the plane. A new feeling of peace swept over me. A sense of forgiveness filled me, and contrary to what you might think the need for revenge went out of me. The resentment I felt towards Japan for so long was suddenly lifted from my heart. I could talk openly about my experiences with the peace of mind I had never known before and I wanted to tell my story.

I returned to the beautiful shores of California and I felt really blessed to live in such a wonderful country. I flew over the welcoming symbol of the west, which was a bridge of beautiful design, the Golden Gate Bridge, which enhances the unmistakable, magnificent outline of San Francisco. What an extraordinary and beautiful city.

It took thirty-nine years, nine months, and two days for the government to give me and the other civilians on Wake Island recognition for our contribution to the defense of Wake Island. I received an official discharge from the United States Navy, the World War II Victory medal, the Asiatic Pacific Campaign medal and the American Campaign medal, and a generous check.

To bring my story to date and make an ending, I must tell you about my family. Dad and Iva had eight children and the family get-together throughout the years looked more like a city convention of sorts.

Skeet married a young lady named Wilma McWilliams while he was still in the Coast Guard and stayed married until he died many years later.

Coley had a busy love life. He had married three times after he was divorced from Rosie. His second wife was named Carol Weston from California. His third wife was named Thelma Peters from Minnesota. His fourth and last wife was named Joyce Madison from California. I knew that Coley had become frugal, but I never realized it had become an obsession. His wives said he was tighter than the bark on a tree.

Red died being a cowboy, something that he loved. Dad died quietly in his bed. Iva is still active and matriarch of the family. As for me after celebrating our fifty-fourth year of marriage I lost the love of my life. Norma fell and broke her hip. She never recovered. Yet all in all life has not been that unkind.

I would like to end my story with a little home-spun wisdom that I believe with all my being. You can always tell a country's values by how they honor their dead. Always remember the men who suffered the hell of war and gave their lives that we might enjoy the freedom we have today. Because of their sacrifice down through the ages America still remains a nation among nations. Never take your freedom for granted. Maintain high ethics and love this country. Do not abuse it and lose it.

GOD BLESS AMERICA AND GUIDE OUR LEADERS.

THE END